ON THE DUNES YOU'LL NEVER FORGET IT.

Novel

MISHA SOMMER

Misha Sommer

On the dunes you'll never forget it.
Novel
Misha Sommer

For my parents

Thanks to Christine, Philippe, Françoise, Hans Paul and all my other
friends

Misha Sommer

On the dunes you'll never forget it.

Novel

ISBN 978-3-9525443-2-7
9 783952 544327 >

Prologue

„As we got farther and farther away, the Earth diminished in size. Finally it shrank to the size of a marble, the most beautiful marble you can imagine…seeing this has to change a man.“
James Irwin, Apollo 15

Chapter One

Earlier, Walser stood outside for a long time, looking at the city lights in the valley. It was drizzling and the night sky was overcast.

Wild animals could be heard from the forest and the air was no more than maybe two or three degrees. He froze, but stayed there for a long time, inhaling deeply the cool, moist air, listening to the sound of the rain and just enjoying the moment.

After a while he went into his trailer, made some tea, wrote his story, and turned on the stove and the television.

* * *

An hour has passed since then, but he is still sitting in front of the television.

Time goes by quickly, too quickly. A short night lies ahead of him and although Walser is tired, he doesn't want to take his eyes off the screen. His caravan is equipped with a modern kitchen and a fully stocked refrigerator: sandwiches, cheese, steaks, vegetables, drinks. Maybe he'll cook something later or prepare a cold midnight snack, but now he wants to watch TV and think about it all.

He is glad that he has satellite reception: over 2000 TV channels. He wants to be an Argus Panoptes and as long as possible he wants to stay awake, because anything else would be a waste.

He looks at the clock: 8:55 pm. *The wild bees of Africa* has just started on BBC. The close-up shows the strange jaws of strange animals, they bite their way through their wax cells in the honeycomb. It's all documented: bees' waggle dance, queen pheromones, royal jelly, etc. Even before the wings of a newly hatched worker bee have unfolded, it begins to clean.

One day the observed swarm of bees is driven out of its hive and perches defenseless on a tree. A starving, soaked dog outside in the thunderstorms could not have caused more regret in Walser than this vulnerable collective of insects. Hours later, the swarm finds asylum in an artificial beehive in the agricultural zone. Months later, they move 40 kilometers further to an olive and cedar forest at the foot of Mount Kenya. Happy end. Walser switches to a crime thriller.

10:11 pm. A program on National Geographic about the Okavango Delta. The voiceover says: "The hippos are creatures of habit". He finds it funny. He learns that the hippos plow their way through the aquatic plants, which in turn helps to get the otherwise stagnant water to flow. They are therefore considered to be the actual architects of this delta, because the water is redistributed due to their beaten path. Thanks to the hippos, the delta does not turn into a salt desert after the dry season: the trailed paths continue to exist and the water then flows precisely through these hollows.

11:05 pm. A karate action film has just ended on the VOX tv channel, followed by a program about animal hybrids: mule, grolar bear, liger, tigon, zebroid, Sheep–goat hybrid, leopon, cama, etc. Funny world, Walser thinks.

He's watched TV so many times in his life, so many hours. The television pictures: compound eyes of humanity. Seen everything a thousand times. There is nothing new. All old hat.

Nothing can surprise you anymore, yes, you've long been an Argus Panoptes, you've seen the world enough, you've seen it to excess. Nobody needs to fool you. It is difficult to give you news.

Walser zaps on the next station: advertising for toothpaste.

11:59 am. He made it to the Fox Movie Channel. They show the Woody Allen film called "Annie Hall" (1977). The main character Alvy Singer is remembering going to the psychiatrist with his mother.

Mother: "He's been depressed. All what he is saying is, that he cannot do anything."

Psychiatrist: "Why are you depressed, Arvey?"

Mother: "Tell Doctor Flicker... it's something he read."

Psychiatrist: "Something you read, huh?"

Boy: "The universe is expanding."

Psychiatrist: "The universe is expanding?"

Boy: "Well, the universe is everything and if it is expanding, someday it will break apart and that will be the end of everything."

Mother: "What is that your business? He stopped doing his homework!"

Boy: "What's the point?"

Mother: "What's got the universe to do with it? You are here in Brooklyn. Brooklyn is not expanding."

12:27 am. He continues to zap on Nat Geo Wild: "Plitvice - In the land of falling lakes." The ancient forests, the clear water of the Cascade Lakes, the fauna. Sadness fills him when he thinks that he wanted to go there two years ago, but had postponed it for the time being because of an important job task he had to implement.

Walser plans to book a trip to Croatia next week.

0:45 a.m. Swiss television. Weather forecast for the next day. Then advertising for the Bernese Oberland in Switzerland and for mineral water from the Graubünden Alps. Later ARTE with animal time: "The Chimpanzees in Gombe", Bavaria 3 with "Journeys to Art: Tuscany". Afterwards, he watches something about Mexico.

1:03 am. *Space Night* on the Bayern Alpha tv channel. It shows the world from above while a spaceshuttle is orbiting the planet. Flight over Alaska, later over Italy. He feels uncomfortable. This is not his cup of tea. Walser switches to a cheaply made action film. He is relieved now, it's good to see people and not the distant surface of a planet. Sometimes cheaply made action films are the best thing in life.

Walser takes a cool can of beer from the refrigerator and then stares at the screen again. If he hadn't gone to that darned Flat Earthers congress a year ago, he could sleep soundly today.

Happy are the ignorant, he thinks and takes a sip of beer.

Chapter Two

THE EARTH IS FLAT.

Bruno Walser stood a little lost in the hotel foyer and looked up at the huge banner that hung from the ceiling. He read the sentence over and over again. The earth is flat, that was so naturally on this banner, as if this was a scientific finding.

Today the third day of the congress of the *Flat Earth Group* took place, a globally ambitious organization, which propagated that the earth is not a sphere, but flat like a frisbee.

Here he felt completely out of place, a reluctant enemy spy. He was not interested in these lowbrows, but someone had to do the dirty work and go to the Flat Earthers Congress. The editorial management of the famous „Zurich Times" had sent him here, even though he usually was responsible for the section "Culture & Arts".

At the editorial meeting, his colleague Huber from the "Research & Technology" section was very reluctant to conduct investigative research himself. That is beneath his dignity, Huber had said, after all, he had a master's degree in physics. Then everyone looked at Walser. He could take over the "impartial" role and should have a closer look at these conspiracy theorists. Walser should show the newspaper readers what kind of people still believe in the flat earth today, in times of electric cars, crypto currencies and Mars missions.

He had already started a conversation with some Flat Flat Earthers and had them explain the world to him. NASA is lying, an elderly lady told him indignantly. They were never on the moon, that was just to win the race against the Russians. A young man, barely twenty, agreed. Yeah, the moon isn't real anyway. The whole universe is fake.

The followers were a very heterogeneous group. Only their belief that the earth was not a sphere but a disk linked them together.

There was a young couple who actually made a reasonable impression apart from their belief in a flat earth though. They had come with their two toddlers. So the next generation of brainwashed Flat Earthers was already there, Walser thought annoyed.

Then the alternative local politician from Graubünden, who wore a T-shirt that said "Forget the globe". A well-known and high level manager from the Basel pharmaceutical industry was there too. She was a lady in her Sixties. She strictly forbade Walser to write a word about her in his article, but told him that she had long since stopped believing in the moon landing and the live photos of the International Space Station. On the other hand, a young ethnology student was more talkative about his belief in a worldwide deception. This way, the governments want to control people, he said.

Walser got along best with the retired master locksmith, who said that he had always been interested in astronomy and that some things just didn't sound right to him. His incentive to join the congress was to investigate and listen to alternative explanations.

Walser passed a sales stand around which a good dozen visitors had gathered. Various Globus alternatives were on the table. He took a snow globe and shook it. Snowflakes fell on the disk of the earth. "Everything is handmade," said the seller proudly. In addition, T-shirts and sweaters with relevant inscriptions:

NASA is lying
The earth is flat
Think for yourself. Question the globe lie

In the large conference room there were already many people talking in groups. Walser tried to overhear some conversations, but it was not possible in the midst of the many voices and the parallel conversations. Suddenly Max Lienhard, the chairman of the Flat Earthers, entered the room. Walser seized the opportunity and fought his way through the crowd to get to Lienhard. Before he could speak to him, two giants, presumably bodyguards, built up in front of him and blocked his way, which did not prevent him from showing Lienhard his press card.

"Mr. Lienhard, my name is Walser and I work for the *Zurich Times*. I would ask you for a spontaneous interview."

Lienhard assessed him and the ID and then nodded in agreement. "Ok, five minutes. Go ahead," said Lienhard. He looked tired and a little absent-minded, but Walser wouldn't underestimate him. One could have a bad opinion about Flat Flat Earthers, but it was known that Lienhard was a smart guy.

"How can someone like you believe in the flat earth?" Walser came straight to the point.

"Someone like me?" Lienhard gave him a stern look.

"How can someone with common sense ignore facts?" Walser insisted. He did not allow himself to be intimidated.

"Prove me wrong." Lienhard looked imperturbable. Walser wanted to provoke Lienhard, but this seemed difficult. The Flat Earthers had an answer for everything.

"Have you never heard of Apollo 11?" asked Walser.

"Who says the moon landing actually took place?" asked Lienhard. Walser was annoyed that Lienhard answered with a counter question. He would still try to bring him out of his shell.

"And the many photos and film recordings: Armstrong in the lunar sand, the raised US flag, the jumps in weightlessness?" Walser asked further.

"Studio recordings can be very convincing", said Lienhard.

"The pictures look damn real", said Walser.

"Have you never seen the movie *2001: A Space Odyssey*? Everything looks damn real. Stanley Kubrick was a genius."

"And the recordings from Mars?" asked Walser. He had to ask these questions in order to better assess Lienhard.

"Look at a photo of *Devon Island,* Canada, and color it red. And here, you have your Martian landscape." Lienhard didn't seem in the least insecure. He seemed certain of his cause.

"And what about the weather satellite, which circled the globe for the first time from a distance of 700 kilometers in 1960 and took the first photo of the globe from space?" asked Walser and could already guess the answer.

"You mean Tiros 1, who made these recordings on April 1st", said Lienhard.

"So you want to imply that it only was a joke because it happened at April Fool's day?" asked Walser, „then also the famous parachute jump from the stratosphere was just a fake according to you. This was a real time TV broadcast straight from the balloon. 39 kilometers above ground. The curvature of the earth was clearly visible to the 2 billion viewers."

Walser was sure that he would find a weak point somewhere in the reasoning of the Flat Earthers.

"Nobody really saw this jump because nobody else was standing with him on the jump ramp. Only a camera was there."

Lienhard was like Teflon.

However, Walser was not surprised by this answer, because he knew that it was extremely difficult to argue with conspiracy theorists. It was tricky to refute their statements as they were often hard to assess. In addition, they simply twisted or denied the facts. Still, he felt a touch of anger. Lienhard couldn't be so brazen. But he was so brazen.

"That stratosphere jump was a nice show," said Lienhard, "financed by a large corporation that sells energy drinks."

Lienhard apparently remained calm. Walser's pulse, however, increased.

"So just a conspiracy?" asked Walser. He had to control himself to remain outwardly calm.

"You can check that for yourself: With a wide-angle lens, every line looks curved, including the horizon," said Lienhard, looking at the clock. "I really have to go now, the lecture ...". He looked impatient.

Walser saw that he would not get any further with his previous questions. He would have to use a different interview strategy to crack Lienhard.

"I would like to understand what was the decisive factor for you personally to turn your back on scientific facts." He had finally found a good starting point. Now he might nail Lienhard.

"I cannot explain that to you in two sentences. Please excuse me now, your five minutes have expired and I have to give my presentation. It is very important." Lienhard's hurry seemed real and he actually seemed under pressure. Nevertheless, Walser was angry and disappointed at the same time, but tried not to let the anger show.

"Later then?" He asked calmly. Now, of all times, when he had found the right questions, Lienhard interrupted the conversation. Presumably that was how he wanted to pull his head out of the noose.

"Yes, all right, let my secretary make an appointment for you." Lienhard pressed a business card into Walser's hand and then hurried to the lectern. The two bodyguards followed him.

The interest in the Flat Earther Conference was great, especially today, because Max Lienhard, as chairman of the up-and-coming Flat Earther movement, was considered the most eloquent speaker here, who, unlike some of his like-minded comrades, argued smart and coherent. This made him credible and ensured him the respect of his opponents.

The Flat Earther movement propagated that the earth was not a sphere, but a flat disk with a transparent sphere, like one of those snow globes that he had shaken earlier. The earth was therefore a kind of inverted frisbee, in the middle of which was the Arctic. The Antarctic, on the other hand, was not an ice desert at the south pole of the globe, but a ring-shaped ice wall of immense dimensions. It was the edge of the frisbee, so to speak, which bordered the oceans, similar to a paddling pool.

During his research, Walser had noticed that it was not that easy to refute the arguments of the Flat Earthers. They just dismissed all photographs and videos of the earth as fakes. Also it was not possible to fly over the Antartica due to some political restrictions. Therefore it was hard to argue about that still quite mysterious place.

The idea of the flat earth seemed absurd, but meanwhile also reputable newspapers were reporting on the movement.

Walser had prepared very intensively beforehand and found out everything available about Lienhard. Little personal information was known about him though. It was said that he was very rich, very smart, that he had made an unquantified fortune with crypto currency. He had traveled a lot in the world. Lienhard was known for being extremely generous. He donated to humanitarian aid organizations and also for environmental protection. There were several foundations, one involved in cleaning up the plastic-contaminated ocean and the other investing in animal welfare. Among other things, Lienhard financed an animal shelter in Crete.

That guy was apparently an honorable man, philanthropist and animal lover, but maybe this was all just a facade. Rumors said that Lienhard was involved in an unsolved murder case and he was even considered as suspect by the police.

Otherwise there was next to no information about him. He was like a phantom. Two years ago he appeared out of nowhere on the scene. He revolutionized the lame Flat Earth organization. Then things escalated quickly and the group became worldwide famous. Just two years ago, the organization held its members' meeting in the adjoining room of the "Hirschen" restaurant, which was located in Adlikon, a village of 600 people in Zurich. Seven interested persons had come at that time. But in the course of these two years the number of members worldwide had grown exponentially and meanwhile it was assumed that they were many million people.

This year's congress took place in the large hall of a luxury hotel in Zurich. The room was designed for more than 500 visitors and was now so overcrowded that people had to stand outside in the corridors and could only watch the lectures on monitors. The event was also broadcast live on the Internet.

Walser was torn between amusement and concern. He had to admit that not all Flat Earthers arguments could be completely dismissed. Some of the criticisms they made were justified, he thought.

In fact, it was strange that historical videos and images of the moon landing were now considered lost. But what made him even more puzzled: Today, more than fifty years after the first moon landing, every cell phone had up to a million times more computing power than the NASA computer at the time. Nevertheless, it was said that lunar missions nowadays were impossible due to technical restrictions. Something indeed was strange.

Lienhard started his talk with the first slide. It showed the well-known "Blue Marble" photo, which was shot in 1972 by the Apollo 17 crew from a distance of 45,000 km. An iconic photo that symbolized the earth. It had been reproduced millions or even billions of times and it was used for a wide variety of media, political and commercial purposes. Lienhard showed the next slide. Again the same picture, but with a disturbing headline: "This is not the earth." Walser had expected stupid statements. However, he felt anger.

The earth is flat, now appeared on the screen. The people cheered, jumped up from their seats and chanted: "The earth is flat! The earth is flat! The earth is flat!"

Instinctively, Walser got up and shouted: "Are you crazy?" But his voice was drowned out in the din of the crowd and he fell silent when he realized that he had lost his composure for a moment. It was his job to report neutrally, but the spectacle made him disgusted. How could Lienhard dazzle people like that? They appeared to him like stupid sheeps.

Finally the crowd calmed down and the lecture continued. Walser was constantly taking notes for the next interview with Lienhard. After half an hour of presentation, he projected some graphics and numbers onto the screen, which again summarized all the criticisms of the sphere model. Then Lienhard took a little dramatic pause and eventually said: "Thank you."

The crowd applauded frenetically and rose again from their chairs. Applause lasted for minutes.

Lienhard suddenly raised his hand, made it clear that the people should sit down and that he wanted to say something else. Immediately the crowd fell silent and listened again to his words. Stupid sheeps, thought Walser.

"There's one more thing ...", Lienhard said and he smiled for the first time that day. The crowd was whispering. Everyone was surprised and excited to see what he would tell.

"I knew it. Now he brings the ultimate proof of the flat earth.", an excited Flat Earther whispered to Walser.

Lienhard called up the next slide: "World sensation. Finally the proof!"

Lienhard wanted to say something, but suddenly a blindingly bright light filled the room near the lectern. A second later there was a loud bang, which was followed by a massive pressure wave that crossed the whole hall and shattered the window panes. The people in the hall were swept from their chairs with great force.

Then silence. There was dust in the air. Walser was on the floor. His ears whistled and his left arm felt awful, but before he could think about it any further, he passed out.

Chapter Three

One year to the day after the attack, on an early Monday afternoon, Bruno Walser was sitting in a Zurich café stirring his latte macchiato. The anniversary of the bomb attack made him pensive.

At this time there was little activity here in the café. Most of the businesspeople had already walked back to work from lunch. Occasionally a few older women sat together by coffee and cake, chatting about their topics.

After the attack on the Flat Earthers Congress, he had been on sick leave during one month, curing his broken arm and his ruptured eardrums.

Meanwhile, the arm only was aching when the weather changed. The ears were ok again. But since he had resumed his work, he preferred to no longer sit in the cramped editorial offices, but rather to look for good stories as a freelance journalist. In addition, he now was responsible for the rubric "Research and Technology" as Huber had resigned his job.

The bomb attack had not yet been resolved. The authorities worked slowly. It had been a miracle that none of the Congressgoers were killed or seriously injured in the attack. Nobody knew anything about Lienhard. It was not even clear whether he still was alive.

Various unconfirmed sources claimed he died of his injuries shortly after the attack. In various Internet forums one could also read about the reasons for the attack. Several conspiracy theories were claiming that it all was because of a secret project that Lienhard had initiated. According to some allegedly leaked reports from from government authorities, Lienhard's team had found the place in Antarctica where the earth's disk ended. Therefore, NASA then wanted to prevent Lienhard from making this public.

There was no official statement from the Flat Earthers, only it was known that Hasler had been elected as the new chairman of the organization. Thanks to the attack there was a new hype.

The theory of the flat earth was discussed everywhere. In contrast to Lienhard, Hasler was an inconspicuous man who acted in the background.

He had rejected Walser's interview request several times. Walser had written a very critical article about the Flat Earthers. Many media cited his report. Afterwards, there was a big resistance against the conspiracy theorist. After various threats, Walser now had a secret phone number and he had also changed his home address.

He was currently working on a multi-part series on the importance of science for science fiction films - and vice versa. His article would treat the question how utopias and futuristic ideas were solidified as new ideas in a society and how they inspired scientists to look for new, sometimes crazy solutions in reality.

Walser's phone vibrated and interrupted his thoughts. The text message came from an unknown number. Apparently someone had done a good job figuring out his secret phone number.

He read the message: *If you want to find out more about the attack on the Flat Earther's conference, then drive to Brunnen which is a resort on Lake Lucerne in Switzerland. Take the cable car up to the mountain station Urmiberg at 9:05 am. Don't tell anyone about it!*

Walser didn't know what to think of it. As a former volunteer in foreign crisis areas, he was fearless enough to put himself in potential danger so that he could get interesting information. He did not believe that any Flat Earther had created a trap for him. Walser did not consider himself to be that important. Nevertheless, he was suspicious and he would leave a message to his apartment in case they should ever look for him.

In any case, it was clear to him that he would accept the invitation and travel to the *Canton of Schwyz* where *Brunnen* was situated. He ordered another coffee and continued writing his science article.

Chapter Four

THE NEXT DAY, WALSER TRAVELED TO *BRUNNEN* AND WENT TO THE valley station of the cable car. It was cool here and the sky appeared gray and impenetrable, like a dome. Walser smiled. Right now, he could almost imagine himself resident of one of the Flat Earther's snow globes that were sold at the congress at the time. Looking now at the landscape that was was surrounding him, he could have even believed in a flat earth.

Here, it all looked so small. It nearly seemed as if the whole world only consisted of this place surrounded by the mountains, *Lake Lucerne* and the advection fog. A paradise for Flat Earthers.

There were no tourists yet. Walser sat alone in the gondola, which leisurely climbed several hundred meters in altitude and at some point also pierced the thick layer of the fog. Suddenly a mighty panorama of the fjord-like mountains and the sea of fog opened up in front of him, which swirled in the shape of Lake Lucerne in the lake basin.

From here nothing definite could be said about the shape of the earth. The landscape looked mountainous, but still like an endless surface, which was now covered by the fluff of the mist. Walser had to blink because the reflection of the sunlight on the white was too bright for the naked eye.

After seven minutes the ride was over, and before Walser even got out of the gondola, he received another text message from unknown: "Now take the footpath to the hiking signs and look under the big stone. Turn off your phone immediately and remove the SIM card. "

Under the said stone, Walser found a cavity in the floor in which a solid plastic box was embedded. He opened it and found a GPS device. As soon as he switched it on, it began to calculate a preprogrammed route. The GPS initially guided him further up the mountain on a hiking trail.

He was sweating as he walked up the steep forest path. Eventually he stopped to take a breather. Through the branches of the trees on the slope he saw the blue of Lake Lucerne.

He had thought a lot about the Flat Earthers since the bomb attack. Most of what this group said he still found stupid. Nevertheless, the attack had also irritated him. This had not been one of those goofy pranks implemented by angry Globe Earthers but a professional and calculated assassination attempt by very dangerous people. It was only by very lucky coincidence that the second bomb had not gone off and that not all of the explosives had detonated on the first bomb. It was obvious: somebody had tried to kill Lienhard at any cost.

But why was he attacked?

Who would benefit from Lienhard's death? Was there a Globe Earther who hated the Flat Earthers so much that he wanted to kill their charismatic boss?

Or a disgruntled astronomer who wanted to save mankind from idiocy?

Or was it perhaps a secret service that didn't want Lienhard to announce something unbelievable like a real proof that the earth actually was flat?

Walser grinned. He imagined an expedition to the edge of the world. A group of adventurers who trudged across the white, seemingly endless ice and snow surface of the Antarctic plateau. Ice cristalls on their beards. Then a sudden stop. In front of them they would see the most extreme abyss in the world. They would stand on that a sharp-edged cliff of ice and instead of the sea, the darkness of the universe would be at their feet: an abyss several billion light years deep that threatened to swallow them up if they took one step too far.

He laughed.

Lienhard's team trudged for weeks across the white, seemingly endless ice and snow surface of the Antarctic plateau. Then eventually they would find the edge of the world. It would be the most extreme abyss in the world. They would stand on that a sharp-edged cliff of ice and instead of the sea, the darkness of the universe would be at their feet: an abyss several billion light years deep that threatened to swallow them up if they took one step too far.

He laughed.

An idiotic idea!

Certainly he didn't take the Flat Earthers seriously, but even when he put aside his reluctance for once and briefly took seriously their conspiracy theories, he couldn't imagine NASA and the governments lying to the people like that. He saw no reasonable motive for this.

These Flat Earthers were not exceptionally intelligent and their judgment could not be trusted blindly. Most of them were just plain ordinary people.

But they weren't stupid either and it struck him as presumptuous to simply portray them as idiots. On the other hand, it contradicted all logic to consider the word of any dilettante as a fact and not to trust the astronomical knowledge that mankind had accumulated over centuries.

Nevertheless, he had to admit that the knowledge he owned was from school books. If he imagined everything for once completely impartially: we were revolving around our sun with thousands of kilometers per hour. It was strange. Also the fact that the sun was a star besides being the bright thing that gave us the normal daylight.

Walser took a deep breath. The air smelled sweetly of drying wood. From the forest path he had a view through the trees to the valley and the lake.

Everything was so calm. No draft here. He tried to imagine how the globe was spinning around itself at 1,670 kilometers per hour. But he felt no movement. Nor did he feel that the earth was right now flying around the sun at around 100,000 kilometers per hour. The idea that the entire solar system was also moving around the core of the galaxy at around a million kilometers per hour was strange.

Nothing of this could be felt here.

A few 100 meters below he saw *Lake Lucerne*, smooth as a mirror. From here the steamers looked like toy ships in a bathtub.

He looked at the scenery for a while.

Then Walser turned around and started moving again on the narrow path, finally reaching a small plateau, from which he followed a hiking trail towards the west. The path tapered more and more and finally guided him through the undergrowth.

After an hour and a half in the zigzag course, Walser finally came to a forest clearing on which there was a somewhat overgrown campsite. *You have reached your destination.* The GPS switched off automatically after the message.

Walser looked around. The place had past its best years. A rusty metal sign with the ordinance on the fire protection law was dated 1986. The fireplace had not been used for a long time. Tangled blackberry bushes and dense nettle plants had almost completely overgrown the heavy grill and the stacked stones, and the wooden bench looked rotten too.

However, the spacious square also offered a remarkable view over the treetops, many of which were already glowing in various shades of red and orange. The whole forest had turned a reddish tinge that tempted the eye to look again and again.

The sun was shining, but the north wind was cooling; a change in the weather was pending. He stood on the sloping edge of the campsite. Shrubs obscured the rugged, rocky end of the terrain, which was pointing steeply several hundred meters into the abyss. This was not a good place for any melancholy.

The fog far below Walser's feet was already full of holes and revealed parts of the green-blue sparkling Lake Lucerne. Here one was embedded in the wild and at the same time lovely landscape. Walser couldn't help but simply absorb this panorama with his eyes for a while.

Then he trudged over the gravel and crossed the campsite. It was noon. At the very edge of the clearing, somewhat hidden, were two caravans, both looking new, both were obviously equipped with solar panels and TV satellite dishes on the roof. So obviously there must have been also a street nearby.

But it seemed that the anonymous host wanted to make sure that nobody could have followed Walser on his way to the secret place.

One of the caravans appeared to be occupied. Steam rose from the vent pipe and it smelled like food. Walser approached that car and knocked.

The door opened and a familiar voice greeted him: "Nice that you are stopping by", the man in the caravan said.

Walser thought: Well, yes! Lienhard lives!

"Please give me your cell phone", continued Lienhard. He seemed to be quite stoic, but was observing Walser with a watchful look. He had grown a beard. There were scars on his forehead and his left cheek and as he made a step ahead he appeared to be limping a little.

When Walser hesitated, Lienhard was energetic: "Now! Your cell phone please!"

Walser gave it to him along with the SIM card. Lienhard took both and put everything in a small box, which he stowed in the trailer.

A pleasant smell of food streamed from the trailer kitchen.

"Come on in, the vegetable soup is ready." Lienhard seemed relaxed again and let Walser enter. In fact, Walser was quite hungry after the march and followed Lienhard into the interior of the car.

Inside it was warm and cozy. The windows were slightly misted up. A television was in the corner and played without sound the BBC News.

Lienhard cut a thick slice from a farmer's bread and handed it to Walser. "Sit down, make yourself comfortable. We'll have a lot to talk about afterwards."

Chapter Five

"WHY AM I HERE?" ASKED WALSER AND TOOK A SIP OF COFFEE.

"I need your help", said Lienhard.

"You know that I don't support your organization." Walser was still amazed that Lienhard of all people had asked him to come here.

"We have similar interests," said Lienhard.

"I'm not sure about that," said Walser, stirring the coffee with a spoon.

"I will tell you everything exclusively, then you can judge for yourself."

Walser just looked at Lienhard and was silent. The whole thing was strange. Lienhard now had to deliver, because this time the constellation was the other way around than at the congress at the time. This time Lienhard was the one asking for a favor.

"Did you know that most Flat Earthers know more about astronomy than most Globe Earthers?" Lienhard asked.

"You mean they know everything about the flat earth?" asked Walser back.

"No, I mean in general they know more: about the size of the earth, the size of the sun, the distances to each other, details about the moon landing, galaxies, the speed of the celestial bodies - all information that one learns in school."

"But the Flat Earthers only learn those things in order to refute the globe earth," said Walser. "And actually, they cannot refute it", he added. He didn't feel like playing the same game as in the first interview with Lienhard.

"See for yourself, let me show you something," said Lienhard. He put a transparent folder with newspaper articles and pictures on the table, then pulled out a picture.

"This is the planet Saturn. Ok?" He tapped the picture. Walser tried to see something suspicious in the picture, but there was nothing. He said, "Yes, I agree, this is Saturn. The picture was made by Voyager 1 in the 1980s if I am right."

"But what is about the colors in this picture? Those brightly colored rings, that blue, yellow, and red of the sphere? Is that what Saturn looks like?" asked Lienhard and vigorously tapped the picture several times.

"What are you getting at?" asked Walser.

"I can't tell you whether Voyager actually flew past Saturn back then. As you know, Flat Earthers doubt anything about NASA. But what I can tell you is that these colors are not real. Even NASA calls the picture a false color photo," said Lienhard.

Then Lienhard leafed through the folder again and looked for another picture that he put on the table. It showed the same planet in a different color. "This is the real Saturn. In real color, as you see it when you look through binoculars or if you fly past it. All in ocher."

"But that doesn't prove that NASA is lying or that the earth is flat."

"No, but it shows that this other picture is an illusion and does not correspond to the facts." Lienhard angrily shook the false color picture.

"What do you mean if you say that it does not correspond to the facts? The false colors are also facts. In this way, the researchers can find hidden information: chemical elements, heat, radiation or other important aspects."

"Yes, but it's about the wrong images in people's heads", Lienhard said urgently.

"But the earth as a disk is also a wrong image," said Walser and wondered what he was doing here.

A year ago this discussion would have been exciting, but now Lienhard was a persona non grata. He was in hiding in the woods and no one asked about him anymore. Why did he even sit here with Lienard? He wondered if he shouldn't just get up and leave.

"Then take a look at the images of the globe, they are all fake. Many were pieced together from thousands of images", said Lienhard.

"A composite picture is by no means misleading," said Walser. He would now allow Lienhard exactly those five minutes that Lienhard had given him back then. If he wasn't satisfied with the conversation after that, he would leave the caravan.

"Often the images of the earth are not even real photos, but illustrations. I made people aware of all these contradictions. But we know how it ended. I was threatened by many haters", said Lienhard. The five minutes were melting.

"But you were not attacked just because you criticize false-color images. Who wanted to kill you and why?" asked Walser.

"Secret services. Because I found something that the world is not allowed to know," said Lienhard.

"And where is your proof of the flat earth then?" asked Walser. He was ready to get up and leave immediately.

Lienhard stood up without a word, opened one of the kitchen cupboards below the sink and bent down. After digging out various cooking utensils and cleaning supplies, he reached for a box at the very back of the closet and pulled it out. It was a small safe that he heaved onto the dining table.

"In here is what you're looking for. A lot of people died for that secret," he said.

Chapter Six

Fifteen years ago nobody would have thought that Lienhard of all people would ever act as the chairman of the Flat Earthers.

He was 30 years old and known at the time as a rational and successful lawyer, an analytical man who did not allow himself to be fooled by anyone, least by some people who claimed that the earth is a disk.

But then everything changed.

It happened while he was sport climbing.

A small carelessness.

The fall lasted a split second.

Then Lienhard's long-term memory was broken.

A week later he would have started working as a partner in a well-known law firm. But now he no longer understood laws and paragraphs because he had forgotten what letters and words were.

And it was even worse:

Lienhard no longer understood the world.

Everything seemed strange to him.

The only good thing about the situation was that he was very smart. He would be able to learn everything again quickly, everyone was sure of that. In addition, it was not ruled out that his long-term memory would function again at some point.

But for now language was of no importance to him. He had to learn it all over again. Only his keen mind would be able to help him fight his way through the hermetic world. He watched TV for hours or he sat outside in the park on a bench and listened to the people in order to catch something of their words and to fathom the meaning.

When he was at home he zapped through the television channels at random. But everything, every picture shown there, everything he saw there, was strange to him, every little thing he had to take out of the abundance and examine carefully. Step by step he had to unravel the world anew for himself.

There was no shortage of progress in the following months and he slowly felt his way back to general knowledge. Lienhard had a crash course about the world thanks to BBC, Discovery Channel and school television and he zapped through all the programs, he read through the Brockhaus and other encyclopedias, almanacs and astronomical yearbooks.

He grabbed his books that had become brittle and dusty from the attic. For whole afternoons he rummaged through old "Readers Digest" and "National Geographic" books, curled by the dampness of the attic. He learned all of this brand new information.

The invention of the Polaroid camera –

The Sputnik flight –

The First and Second World War –

The moon landing –

He also borrowed dozens of nature film videos from the libraries and spent hours watching animal documentaries and travelogues.

So he got to know the life of the gorillas and actually he also got to know that Gorillas existed and what they were because he had forgotten all of this.

Little by little, he heard about the four seasons and about continents, about the Eiffel Tower, about a country called France, about cars and airplanes and also about the journeys of Columbus and Magellan. He heard about Copernicus and Einstein, he read books such as "The Swamp Plants in northern Zurich" and "Our Solar System", he got to know Max Frisch and Goethe, the theory of evolution, he understood the difference between the Arctic and the Antarctic, he studied the animal species like a madman, he practiced algebra and learned the structure of the flower. He read a lot about the history of Switzerland, he learned about the dinosaurs, birds, crocodiles, giraffes, Romans, Greeks and so on.

He was astonished to learn that it all started with amino acids and that maybe a billion years ago only single-cell and multicellular cells called Chlamydomonas, Gonium, Eudorina and Volvox were loitering on earth.

When he saw a baby for the first time, he initially believed he was getting to know a new category of living beings, because he had also forgotten the process of aging and dying and initially found it very strange and, to be honest, he found it also very disturbing. He thought that this might be only one possibility among many others.

Otherwise he found the concept of earth or space strange and unsettling. It appeared strange to him that mankind was stuck on a ball - like ants on a piece of wood in the sea.

Other things he took surprisingly calmly (yes, the earth would one day be a sizzling marshmallow in the sun fire, but only in several billion years, which at least wouldn't bother him and his contemporaries luckily - thanks to the other horrible concept called death.)

For the first time in his life he ate an apple. He did everything for the very first time, heard about everything for the first time, saw it for the first time. He found his own shadow strange, as well as all sorts of noises such as the rustling of packets of biscuits or the rattling of motorcycles, the gurgling of water when pouring into a jug.

Once, when he was sitting by the river, in one of the parks in Zurich, two little boys had to calm him down because a thunderstorm broke out over the city with a great roar and he hadn't known anything about thunderstorms. -

He learned:

Giraffes have long necks,
Elephants are gray, have a long trunk.
Zebras have stripes.
Chameleons change their color.
Magpies steal glittering objects.
Sunflowers align themselves with the light.

After a few months, his level of knowledge roughly matched that of an average person and he was even able to drive a car again. But Lienhard had a new problem now.

Chapter Seven

Lienhard just couldn't cope with this new world. In the past few months he had patiently listened to the many stories that the people and the lexicon had presented to him. He knew what bananas were or the rainforest and that there were other countries.

He also knew that there was a globe and that it was divided into the various continents and seas.

But since his accident he had only known most of these objects from hearsay, or from television, or from pictures, and a lot of it struck him as absurd. In the end, these were all just claims and images, and who could proof that they were true?

He realized that his newly acquired knowledge did not satisfy him at all.

Fine, he knew the content of the Brockhaus Encyclopedia almost by heart, knew exactly what the objects named in it were talking about in terms of the definitions, he also understood their functionality. So he knew, for example, how photosynthesis or an internal combustion engine works. Also did he knew a lot about philosophy and math, but he hadn't seen much with his own eyes.

Much was still alien to him.

Now, a year after the accident, even simple foods were sometimes a mystery to him because he had never tasted them.

For example, the season for elderberries, quinces, lingonberries and chestnuts had not yet started and he knew nothing about them but theory. In all theoretical knowledge, however, Lienhard was very deft: thanks to his books, he knew the historical route of the apricot from China to India, Greece, Italy and America. He even knew about mycres, limonene, p-cymene, terpinolene, α-terpineol and other chemical compounds that marked out their typical taste, but in fact, he had never tasted an apricot. Sure, it was good to know that the taste of a cherry was based on benzaldehyde. Yet he didn't know what a cherry tasted like because he hadn't tried one yet.

The ancient Greeks had a more precise name for the types of knowledge. They called the acquired knowledge, what one could know after reading a dictionary or learning the theory, as *Doxa*. But there was also *Episteme*. It meant that one had really recalculated and checked something and therefore knew. Furthermore, it also required *Gnosis* which only could be attained if one had really experienced something physically and seen it with one's own eyes.

So what value could his knowledge have if physical objects, which he had not seen himself, seemed distant and implausible to him?

But if he hadn't yet had the opportunity to try a fresh apricot or cherries, at least these were not out of the world. It would have been easy for him to somehow find them out of season if he really wanted to. And of course he would also be able to travel and then see the different countries or animals that seemed odd to him (e.g. kangaroos). This certainty calmed him down.

Of course, he would encounter some things himself over time and then he would be able to convince himself of the existence of these things.

His problems, however, were more complex.

There was this strange disbelief, because against better knowledge he just couldn't believe that these things and beings really existed out there: elephants, galaxies, stalactite caves. Ok, elephants and stalactite caves would be accessible. But how was he to proceed with galaxies?

All objects that he had heard about for the second time after his amnesia were just legends for him, because he only knew almost everything from books or television.

This two-dimensionality limited him and he hated that he knew a lot again in terms of Doxa, but still didn't really know it in terms of Episteme and Gnosis. Meanwhile, he had begun to jot down things in a little book. So he noted everything that seemed remarkable to him. He wrote for example:

We tan our skin on a star.

Grazing cows: strange creatures that feed themselves in the way they are used to.

We are all ships-of Theseus-paradoxes

The evening sunlight falls on a skyscraper, the home of the currently predominant species.

But he soon stopped doing it, because in the end pretty much everything seemed strange to him. We had insects make a sticky sweetener from bee pollen for us. We were frying the meat of bulky grass-eaters according to optimized cooking levels, we were cultivating cereals and creating artificial intelligence, we had accidents with leased cars, we explored quantum mechanics and we sat drunk in a bar.

We were darned clever species, that was good to know, but somehow ist also was strange to be part of it.

While shopping in the shopping center, he watched the mothers pushing their babies in their strollers and patting them: brood care. We were smart monkeys, but it was kind of ok. Yes, we were idiots who cheerfully exterminated the plant and animal species and let children play next to buried chemical waste, but somehow he was grateful for this life.

Even when he looked in the mirror, he found it strange how we all looked: our two eyes, iridescent marbles, further that strange little fringe of hair on the frontal bone, those brows. Then the nose with the two holes, also our mouth, this strange hole in which food was introduced and which uttered some sounds. Our lack of fur compared to other mammals, it was weird.

He had gotten used to all of this again, albeit not permanently, because from time to time he felt strange again about it. He did not talk with others about it. At least he was able to look at himself calmly and say to himself again and again: That's the way it is, that's how we are. Maybe he just had to come to terms with the oddity of the world and get back to everyday life.

But still: many things eluded Lienhard's observation or were at least difficult to find. For example, recently he had seen a rainbow over Zurich and he admired the beauty of this prism so much, hoping to see a rainbow again with every rain. But this did not happen. And also it would not cover all types of rainbows either.

He would probably never see with his own eyes a Moonbow, a Circumhorizontal arc, a Dewbow or even a Fogbow. Probably he also would never see an Interference Rainbow or a red Rainbow that worked like a dawn or a sunset. Sighting a Double Rainbow in general and a Twinned Rainbow in particular was tricky, and sighting a White Rainbow was almost impossible. Lienhard had read that only with a lot of luck one would be able to ever see a Full-circle Rainbow from a helicopter or a mountain. For such special, rare events, many factors were required. So he skipped any attempt, because else he would have been obliged to make this aim the only task in his life.

He would also not become an expert in each field, because no matter in which direction his interest would develop, his endeavor would automatically be doomed to failure. He did not even have to start with certain topics. Anyway, each attempt would be just a mockery in comparison with the real amount of possibilities. The abundance of the world was too powerful for one person alone.

Certainly, in the past few months he had come into direct contact with many generic representatives and their derivatives and variations, a few thousand objects from everyday life. It costed him no effort.

He just came in contact with those objects very naturally during his everyday life (city, house, street, traffic light, computer, rain, metal, sugar beet, honey, chicken egg, house cat, dog, train station, awning, chocolate, colors, smells, peanut, tram, shoe, supermarket, car, etc.), but a lot of things were missing.

It was about objects that could be seen only rarely for example due to seasonal appearances: snow, cocoa beans, wild cats, volcanoes, airports, palm trees, hail, twins, forests, shooting stars, sea, etc.

He would either have to wait for it or he would have to proactively seek out immovable objects. In addition, there were the many unique items (e.g. certain towns, lakes, mountains, countries, etc.).

The whole thing was also relativized by the question of what he really wanted to see. There were also many objects that he had not even seen with his own eyes before his amnesia (e.g. Brazilian rainforest, Sugar beet, etc.) because they did not matter for him.

What person could ever claim to have seen and experienced most of the objects on earth?

Besides the sheer abundance of things in this world, there was something else that annoyed him. He had almost accepted the fact that there were too many objects in terms of amount of things. What bothered him even more was rather that there also were things he would never see them due to other reasons. He became very dissatisfied with it and began to set up a system of those objects that he could see with his own eyes and those that he would never see, at least not directly:

		Tangibility (temporal, spatial) and visibility (live, immediate)			
		(1) easy	(2) somme effort	(3) immense effort and / or by chance	unreachable
Number	**(A) Unique**	e.g. the Self (psych.)	e.g. Paris Eiffel Tower, rare natural phenomena	e.g. celebrities, originals of some famous works of art	e.g. in general the past & future, the star XY, Pangäa
	(B) small contingent	e.g. range of experienced feelings	e.g. the animals in a particular zoo	e.g. rainbow types, in the near future: Mars, orbiting the moon	e.g. other planets in our solar system
	(C) large contingent	e.g people you get to know in the course of life	e.g. all Starbucks coffee outlets worldwide	e.g. types of Fanta cans ever made from every country around the world	e.g. galaxies
	(D) immense contingent	e.g. all groceries in a large delicatessen store	e.g. all Swiss apple varieties, all towns in Switzerland	e.g. fruit varieties in the world, each of the 6,800 Swiss communities, every hiking trail in Switzerland, 76,562 km of the Swiss road network	e.g. stars, dimensions, Planck sizes, presumed parallel universes, processes and elements on the quantum level
	(E) infinite	n.a	n.a	n.a	totality of everything in the absolute broadest sense; even subsets: e.g. list of all numbers in an infinite mathematical series (cardinal numbers, etc.), any multiverses, dimensions , etc.

If he wanted to visualize objects and make direct contact with them, he would only be able to cover area A1 to D3, but only incompletely. All of this would inevitably remain incomplete, he knew that very well: as soon as the population of all objects in a certain category had reached a certain size, it was automatically clear that he would only see a small percentage of them himself, even though the number of objects was ultimately finite.

In addition, it did not end with finite and yet indomitable quantities, because it never ended, but became even more numerous and difficult to reach, until it finally ended at E4 in infinity and inaccessibility.

Certainly, in the future there would be shifts in those areas for humans: Perhaps one day time travel, wormholes and other things would be accessible by humans. However, he would have to come to terms with the fact that at the current point in time he would never be able to see the objects in these areas with his own eyes. The current state of science could not have enabled even the richest person in the world to see anything in column 4 up close with their own eyes.

Chapter Eight

The unattainable preoccupied him. He lacked direct intuition and both, complex and very banal things mad him skeptical.

He simply doubted everything that he had not yet seen, felt and experienced and that would not be available to him in the future either.

Everything would remain just a legend until he verified it himself.

He recently came across the concept of evidence ("*pro ommaton poiein*") in a rhetoric book and this concept seemed correct to his current situation.It also matched with the idea of Episteme and Gnosis.

So now, he decided that he would experience the world firsthand. He already knew the limitations, but he felt the desire to at least see as much as possible live and with his own eyes. Nothing should remain a legend, everything should be freed from its 2D situation.

Otherwise, how should he be able to believe that there was Saturn and Jupiter and how should he ever really imagine their size and grandeur if he only knew them from pictures and would never be able to see them for himself?

Everything was so strange, but what almost irritated and bothered him the most was that he seemed to be the only person who was amazed at all of this. This is what he could understand least of all.

Because after his Second Age of Enlightenment, as he now jokingly called the time of re-learning, he quickly noticed that no one else was surprised about the strangeness of the world.

Even he felt strange about the world only from time to time. Everything, the whole world, was a kind of ambiguous image for him and he wavered between acceptance and disbelief. And when he opened one of his books again ("From the caterpillar to the butter-fly", "The cow and its 4 stomachs"), he gazed at the pictures and explanations and felt nothing but an unsatisfactory emptiness.

But when he asked his friends about it, their answer was always the same. How should it be otherwise, they said. Yes, you are right, but it cannot be dealt with all the time. Don't be eccentric. Finally turn to normalcy, weirdo!

But he couldn't. He was stuck.

Chapter Nine

THE ATTEMPTS OF HIS FRIENDS TO BRING LIENHARD TO REASON DID not help and he could not allay his concerns.

He stood in his study and looked perplexed at the book spines on the shelf, read the titles of those books that had taught him so much in the past few months.

The big book of spices, The big book of exotic species, Fruits from the tropics and subtropics, All about the even-toed ungulates, The tree varieties of the north, The big book of vegetables from all over the world, Our solar system, Characters and alphabets of all times and peoples, Descriptive statistics, Inductive Statistics, Lunar Atlas, Malta in three days, etc.

Then he took the book from the shelf that once had been the most important book of the world for him: *The Brockhaus encyclopedia in one volume*, a giant lexicon which, after his amnesia, had brought the world closer to him in alphabetical order.

That book had been a pathfinder for him, it had helped him to find a way through the confusing world.

At that time he had read the book page by page. But now this was no longer enough for him. Now it was about the search for the moment in which something became true for him from a mere image. And for that he would have to visualize everything he could.

An efficient, economical approach was required and he would come up with rules that could help him to limit the scope of his endeavor. So he basically decided to see as much with his own eyes as an average citizen of today's Europe would have seen at the same age.

He looked back at the Brockhaus, held the heavy, thick book in his hands, leafed through it a little, then let the pages jump like in a flip book and the terms from Z to A passed faster and faster:

... interest ... superconductivity ... pony ... council ... Jupiter ... chrysanthemum ... Brindisi ... acacia ...

Then he closed the book again. *The Brockhaus encyclopedia in one volume* comprised 1019 pages and it had cost him a lot of effort in the past few months to work through all the theoretical explanations.

Accordingly, it now seemed illusory to him to look at every object from the Brockhaus, unless he was proceeding very system-atically.

So in a first step he organized all the terms the Brockhaus book was containing according to categories, accepting thematic overlaps and methodological inaccuracies.

So he finally defined 16 categories from all the subject areas and then randomly assigned a color to each of them:

- 1. Yellow: culinary (e.g. marzipan)
- 2. Orange: nature (e.g. mastodon)
- 3. Signal red: unit of measurement (e.g. March)
- 4. Wine red: philosophy (e.g. power)
- 5. Pink: technique (e.g. burl)
- 6. Pink: infrastructure (e.g. sailor)
- 7. Violet: economy (e.g. Strait of Magellan)

- 8. Light gray: legal system (e.g. measures)
- 9. Dark gray: linguistics (e.g. Mandarin)
- 10. Beige: person (e.g. Marx)
- 11. Dark green: architecture (e.g. attic)
- 12. Olive green: cultural (e.g. mask)
- 13. Braun: history (e.g. Machiavelli)
- 14.Light green: geography (e.g. Monaco)
- 15. Dark blue: astronomy (e.g. moon)
- 16. Light blue: miscellaneous (e.g. pig)

Then he went through the book page by page and with felt-tip pens he color-coded each term.

He soon saw that he could exclude some of his arbitrarily chosen categories. Either some of the included terms were referring to objects that were incorporeal, theoretical (e.g. terms within the category "philosophy" such as "epistemology", " existentialism", or "discourse".). So he had already worked through them already anyway. Or aside from that, many of these topics had a complex tree structure. For example, physics ("nature") was divided into various subtopics, for example mechanics, which in turn covered statics, dynamics and kinetics. He would only follow such systems to a limited extent.

In any case, he was able to largely delete the categories of "philosophy", "legal system", "linguistics", "person", "history", "unit of measurement" and "economy" – with some exceptions. For example, if he were to visit Rome in the context of "geography", it was clear that the categories "history", "people" and "culture" were also connected to it. He handled this and other overlaps willingly and generously. He also defined three exclusion criteria:

1. *I won't look for anything that comes to me (e.g. animal species that are "automatically" to be found in Switzerland anyway: domestic cat, blackbird, Pigeon, heron, red kite, stork, hedgehog, fox, mouse, ant, etc.)*

2. *I will only work through the almost infinite number of variants of an object as long as I enjoy it and as it still refreshes me and makes me happy.*
3. *No obnoxious objects and facts*

In addition, he renounced to know all the variations of an object, at least he would not aim for it in every case. Anyway, he would approach everything as pragmatically as possible.

Therefore he had assigned each object to only one category, otherwise there would have been constant overlaps between the categories. He accepted that the assignment of the terms to the categories he had chosen was ultimately arbitrary and not conclusive.

With all those considerations, he'd cut his to-do list by about 50 percent. So these were his tasks, which he would work through very systematically as best he could.

Of course, this strict concept was not always actionable. Sometimes he also had to be spontaneous.

Later, when he was working in the middle of the "Geography" category and was staying in South Africa for this purpose, he had to organize a spontaneous trip to Bonn. Because there, in the botanical garden, was a titan arum. This had just started to bloom, which only happened every few years and lasted only a few days.

Chapter Ten

In a first step of his *Brockhaus* project, he took on the category "culinary" and looked at his long task list. At some point, he ad given up his wish to have tasted all the fruits and vegetables in the world completely because many species existed and there was also a a huge variety of types.

20,000 varieties of apples

90 types of coffee

100,000 rice varieties

400 dessert and fruit-banana varieties

There were around 100 species of peas worldwide and around 2,000 varieties of mint. Incidentally, the world's largest seed bank with 860,000 varieties was stored in a vault in Svalbard.

So he could dwell on the culinary topic as long as he wanted and still would get nowhere. Just for fun and curiosity, he still wanted to deal with it for a while.

He had already worked out a minimalistic plan of automatically doing "field research" in the supermarkets by purchasing all offered types of fruits and vegetables: *orange, lemon, banana, kiwi fruit, kumquat, grapefruit, physalis, carambola, cherimoya, avocado, coconut, plantain, persimmon, avocado, kiwano, guava, passion fruit, pomegranate, papaya, prickly pear, guava, pomelo, carambola, pitahaya and cherimoya.*

For the more sophisticated portfolio, he contacted world-famous food scouts in various countries and had them send him samples of new fruits and vegetables.

In specialized online shops he also got less well-known things like the *Indian banana*, which outwardly resembled a pale green mango and combined the taste of mango, apricot, pineapple and vanilla.

He also got *lime finger* there, a small citrus variety from Australia. It was shaped like a *kumquat* that had turned out too long and instead of orange it was colored green-brown or rather pink. When it was cut in half, small balls oozed out. These sour globules could be drizzled on salmon. They bursted like caviar, with a sour, sweet taste that somehow felt lighter than the one of a normal lemon.

On his later travels he also visited many local markets and tasted all kinds of exotic varieties, *jackfruit, pandanus, tomatilla, akebia, salak, buriti fruit, horn cucumber, monkfruit, curuba, nashi, cape gooseberry, loquat, java apple, nashi, rambutan, tomatillo, tamarillo, carob, baobab* and a lot of nameless things. He tried thousands upon thousands of fruits and vegetables from all over the world and despite all his good intentions of not to yaw after the abundance, he celebrated the variety to the point of excess. It took him six months to achieve notable achievements.

But more and more the versions of a single genus also began to appeal to him and he tried the 3,000 varieties of the potato, later he liked the apple theme:

Ananas Reinette
Basler Winterapfel
Bänziger
Blauacher Wädenswil
Chüsenrainer
Dülmener Herbstrosenapfel
Gelber Richard
Winterapfel

By chance he found out about a guy in Austria who cultivated thousands of chilli varieties in his fields and asked him to show him the variants.

Addicted to the varieties, Lienhard went on and on, also ate his way through the tomato varieties, black, pink, yellow, purple, green, big, small, sweet, spicy. He memorized their taste.

After having worked through so many foods and food plants, at some point he had to admit that he had now deviated from the *Brockhaus encyclopedia* path. He had to get back to his goal. His conclusion: within six months he had just explored the variations - or at least a large part of them - of three objects (chilli, tomatoes and potatoes). As expected, even the apple had overwhelmed him and he hadn't even been able to try half of all apple variations. He would now try again to continue on his *Brockhaus* path and not drift too far away. In the future, random samples would have to be sufficient as example for all other varieties.

In the following months he devoted himself to new culinary endeavors and dealt with a wide variety of delicacies from *black garlic* and *manna* to the various types of honey, salt and mustard. He was interested to taste anything including lemon thyme tea. He might not like it, just as he hadn't liked the chrysanthemum juice that he had discovered in the Asian shop.

But he knew he would love both as much as he loved tomatoes and chilli. He wanted to feel the variety, all the permutations of the aroma, he deeply felt the desire to have tried almost everything once, he wanted to know from personal experience how brown caramel cheese from Norway tasted.

He wanted to feel the variety, all the permutations of the aroma, he deeply felt the desire to have tried almost everything once. So he wanted to know from personal experience how brown caramel cheese from Norway tasted or how sweet the sweetest sugar of the world could be or the hottest chilli ever.

Yes, he wanted to feel the variety, all the permutations of the aroma. But one day he definitely gave up his active occupation with the category "culinary ", otherwise he would have had to devote his whole life to this topic alone and this would have been too one-sided for him, because the rest of the *Brockhaus* list was large. Therefore he wasn't going to follow this culinary rabbit hole anymore. Indeed, he was crazy, but not completely stupid.

But still he was gripped by a longing for the whole world, for every detail. The desire to know everything, to try everything, all the smells and tastes of this earth, took possession of him.

He wanted everything, was that too much?

The longing to know every fruit, every plant, every animal, but also every country, every village, every piece of earth, every cave, every centimeter in the sea, every moment, to be able to look at everything in slow motion and fast motion.

He wanted nothing less than the whole world.

Chapter Eleven

AFTER HE HAD INCOMPLETELY FINISHED THE SUBJECT OF "CULINARY", he turned to the "nature" category. He was approaching the topic step by step and with the given restrictions and rules.

First he went to the Zurich Zoo. Certainly, again this was a boldness. This visit was ridiculous in relation to all animal species. According to the lexicon, so many species were currently known: 5,501 mammals, 6,771 amphibians, 9,547 reptiles, 10,064 birds, 32,400 fish, 47,000 crustaceans, 85,000 molluscs, 102,248 arachnids, 71 '000 other lower animals and more than 1'000'000 insect species. Not to speak of individuals of any kind.

Also not included were all the undiscovered species that were already extinct again and the marine animals that we did not yet know and perhaps would never get to know. The UN estimated that 50 animal and plant species became extinct - every day!

Many of them without ever being discovered by us.

But even so, in just one day, he saw almost 400 species of animals at once in this only zoo. With that he had probably covered a large part of all animals that an average person would ever see in his life, although of course the zoos in each country were configured differently and stocked with different animals.

During his zoo visit, he also looked at a tapir for the first time and he thought: what a strange creature! Then he went to the giraffe enclosure and observed these strange animals with their long necks. But he was even more amazed at the zoo visitors who looked at these creatures very calmly. The people were so relaxed. For them, everything was so normal. Only their children were excited and surprised about the strange creatures in the zoo. But then he went to the kiosk, bought a vanilla ice cream like the children and while he was eating it, he walked past the various animal enclosures and thought: It is the way it is, why not?

Then it was the turn of the next sections of his to do list. Everything step by step and with the given restrictions and rules.

Earth, beloved peacock, keep showing your feathers.

Chapter Twelve

TRULY, THE CATEGORY "NATURE" IN THE CONTEXT OF LIENHARD'S *Brockhaus* activities was a huge topic and he toiled with it for many months, but at some point he had seen enough. Again it was just a ridiculous part, but enough to be satisfied.

But he had more and more doubts as to whether he was on the right track.

He had sacrificed so much time for his activities: three full years had passed since his accident in which - despite all the busyness - he had not been employed by anybody.

Certainly, he had been smart and had taught himself to trade on the stock exchange in the "Economy" category. But althought he had made a fortune trading securities, and later also cryptocurrency, that didn't count.

His reputation was ruined, his career ended before it really started. Many friends had turned away from him because he had not listened to their advice and had not followed normalcy.

When winter comes after an eventful year and you are at the beginning of the journey, of a sabbatical, when you know something new is going to come, even you still don't know what it will be, then it is chic to stroll pensive through the streets - through the fog of time.

You see boys throwing snowballs at the tram windows.

Their laughter in timeless times: contagious.

They are looking forward to future heroics.

But one spring, summer, autumn and winter later, when the snow falls through a white wall of sky, again, and then you roam around, again, still ... still without an official job, but with a project in your head. Ideas that you believe in, but nobody else does. Actually because you haven't told anyone about it.

Nobody would accept it anyway. So if at that moment your sabbatical contingent has long been used up, when it is running on reserve.

All the goodwill of your friends and your family are used up. No one even talks anymore about your absence from the everyday life, nobody even asks you what you are doing all day or what your achievements of the day were.

This frozen time.

And then you sit again in the tram in the new winter: again snowballs hit the window, thrown by the same boys or maybe others, again their laughter: a laugh that never ages and that is detached from time. It can extract your youth out of your body if you just stand still long enough.

Lienhard was outlawed and he knew. As before, he was convinced of his secret agenda and believed that his goal could ultimately be of use. In his opinion, he was not a good-for-nothing, but rather occupied a niche that had to be filled by someone because someone had to do it. Someone had to be the person who, as an adult, walked this strange path and looked at the world for the first time with an emptied, but at the same time docile look.

Now he had come to "geography". He could combine it very well with other categories such as important personalities (e.g. Platon, Napoleon, Van Gogh), architectural masterpieces and culture in general. But he wondered if he could somehow shorten the whole thing and if there wasn't a trick to literally not have to go to every country and to see every landmark with his own eyes.

But pictures, videos or Google Street View would not be enough, because he had already used them enough for Doxa. He knew that he could only honestly believe that "Paris", "Tokyo", "Rome", "New York" did not just exist in pictures but were real - that they were accessible places - if he had really seen these places with his own eyes.

So he had to go out into the world to free the legendary landmarks of metropolises and countries from their two-dimensionality. Only then would a picture become true: when he had really visited a distant place that he would otherwise not believe existed.

But maybe it would be enough if he only freed a handful of the most important landmarks in the world from their flat existence in pictures. Maybe even a single landmark would be enough for a whole country. Or maybe a single landmark could be the deputy for all other landmarks. He could possibly just look for a single iconic landmark in reality and then infer all the others from it.

He thought of Paris.

After Lienhard decided to travel to Paris, he immediately took the next train. At first he thought to himself: until I have seen the Eiffel Tower, I will not be able to believe that I am in Paris. Only then did I arrive in this city, really arrived.

But when he actually saw the Eiffel Tower, behind the roof of a building, this sight didn't remind him of anything majestic, but rather of the mast of an overland power line. The Paris within the picture books was not the Paris he was now finding.

He was disappointed. Working through the "geography" was not as easy as the other categories within the *Brockhaus*. Something was preventing him from arriving in Paris.

Nevertheless, he approached the metal structure, sat down on a park bench in front of it. Then he recognized the size, the art of the architecture: what a wonderfully lavish construction!

And although he still didn't know whether he found the Eiffel

Tower beautiful or ugly, he realized at that moment that he was on the trail of a discovery.

He decided that he would not stop traveling until he understood the mechanics of traveling. Now he wanted to find out how long it took before he really felt he had arrived at a place. What did it take to free a travel destination from its two-dimensionality?

So to say, he wanted to step into the picture and become part of the place, not just be a viewer, a bystander.

Chapter Thirteen

AFTER HIS AMBIVALENT VISIT TO THE EIFFEL TOWER, HE DECIDED TO
go to a place that was smaller than Paris, but without a particular
landmark that caught the attention of tourists. He wanted a city that
was viewed more as a total work of art and not as the home of a
specific landmark or a strong focal point of tourist longings. That
place should be rather a conglomerate of many small elements that
together made a whole.

So he booked three nights in Venice starting the next best day.
For a lot of money he took a room in a completely snobbish hotel
right on the Grand Canal. Three full days would be enough for his
mission. On average, tourists only stayed in Venice for two days.

The following day, Lienhard was in Venice.

His tourist boat drove along the stakes to the island of Burano,
the island with the colorful fishermen's houses and the sweet dough
rings. The gray sky merged seamlessly into the gray of the sea.

Later, at the Rialto Market, a man peeled artichokes in pieces and
threw the finished pieces into a bucket of water.

In the side streets of Venice the laundry was drying in the sun, a
canopy of clothes like an art installation.

The bright red hydrants stood out nicely from the vintage walls and even the garbage disposal with the garbage bags in the wheel-barrows was worth seeing. Lienhard found it almost annoying how photogenic everything presented itself and occupied him. And if something was so ugly that even the biggest Venice fan could not have denied it, then the beautiful often did not stay away, so that the two extremes again resulted in an advantageous contrast and the ugly only flattered the beautiful again.

Venice was an imposition in everything. Because even if Lienhard would have known all the streets of Venice, all the canals, all the buildings, Venice was still everywhere and nowhere. The many aspects of Venice strained him and Lienhard felt lost because basically he should have photographed or filmed everything like Google Streetview. Everything was pointless in view of the many possibilities. Lienhard degenerated into Sisyphus. On the other hand, things were gradually repeating themselves.

On the first day he had automatically started to categorize things: bridges, canals, alleys, houses, courtyards, restaurants. He paid attention to the differences (length, width and shape of the alley, specifications of the bridge railings, etc.) and special features (e.g. the highest house number: No. 6828).

After he had apparently largely browsed everything according to the travel guide, his next goal was to see what residual benefits the place could still offer.

However, Lienhard found that this new kind of boredom had not followed the well-being of having seen everything he needed. On the contrary: nothing had been finished. He had checked off many sights, but it seemed to him that these were not the essentials.

In any case, he did not have the desired effect.

As on the day of his departure, he walked to the train station, he glanced one last time from the bridge over the Grand Canal and the vaporetti in the morning light, and all of a sudden he remembered all those activities that he had completely forgotten to implement: a ride early in the morning with the very first vaporetto on line 1 - the whole Descend the canal. Or he could have eaten *Tramezzini* and *Baccalà Mantecato*. Also he could have visited the island of

Torcello. Further he could have strolled on the 12 km long sandy beach of the Lido island.

And yet he could have boasted in front of his friends that he had visited Venice and no one could have denied this, only himself.

He spontaneously decided not to leave Venice. Instead, he would stay in Venice until he found what he was looking for.

He then asked a waiter in the station café to recommend a cheap hotel. Lienhard booked it for ten days.

* * *

The lobby smelled of cheap vanilla room scent when he entered. The concierge, a young, lanky guy, no more than twenty years old, greeted him: "Welcome to Venice".

Lienhard checked in and got to work. In the days that followed, he caried out all the tourist-activities that had occurred to him on the morning of the supposed farewell.

Meanwhile, he had bought five different city maps and a compass. Now it wouldn't happen to him anymore that he got lost in the alleys of Venice. The first map showed all the buildings in three dimensions. The second map showed the islands not only as abstract squares and circles, but also in their actual shape and also in geographical relation to Venice itself.

Even lesser-known islands could be seen. The third map showed the detailed ferry routes, but was unwieldy. The fourth map turned out to be useless. But then he thought: super tourist map, where have you been all this time? Tourist map number five was amazing. It not only showed the quarters in different colors and the names of the quarters, but also marked the "highways" through Venice in yellow.

It was wonderful.

Immediately he took his first test walk.

In the far north of the island, on the seashore, he came to an astonishingly unadorned residential area. The makers of his obsolete map hadn't bothered to record this corner of Venice as well. In fact, it had concealed this place. Instead it was covered by an information box ("Your exclusive discounts in Venice restaurants"). Lienhard found it funny: if the city map ended where a tourist wanted to continue, if this area one was visiting no longer belonged to the city's certified tourist area.

Then one got into no man's land, so to speak, terra incognita.

But now things had changed: his new super map, on the other hand, showed this part of Venice.

Lienhard asked himself, however, whether this was even necessary. Did he really have to know every detail for the overall picture, when probably not even the real Venetians knew every corner, every alley, every canal of their city.

He passed a businesswoman on the phone: "Pronto-pronto .... io ti senti, tu mi senti? ... Pronto ?? ... Ah? .... Eco dimi ... pronto ... certo, ma certo ... ".

Lienhard marched on. Through the bars of a massive gate he saw a beautiful garden, which he found rather demoralizing though. The best city map couldn't help him. The real Venetians were shy deer who followed their secret paths and protected their private gardens from the eyes of tourists. So Lienhard knew that the city would ultimately remain hermetically to him: as a tourist in Venice, he would always remain an outsider and would merely stroll through a Potemkin village.

He could only ever get to the surface, which was very soft, but underneath was the private Venice, the inner granite, the real Venetian life left exclusively to the locals.

Finally he spotted something authentic, real as he arrived at the café south of the Fondamente Nuovo. There, the vaporetto captains got their snacks and exchanged a few words with the employee. He loved to watch them unobtrusively.

* * *

After ten days, Lienhard left the hotel on St. Mark's Square. Instead, he found a place to stay in a huge flat of an older single lady, Signora Rigozzi. For 60 years, she already had been living here, on the edge of the Castello quarter. She was one of the remaining locals in Venice.

Nobody was waiting for her on the mainland and she did not want to go to a retirement home either, although she was already 93 years old. She rented out a room with a private bathroom and he was allowed to use her kitchen.

Often she cooked for both of them and then they ate together at the small table that was covered with a flowerish wax-blanket. Then she told him with wet eyes about Venice in the 1940s, when she worked as a young girl in the Fenice Theater. Sometimes she even invited him to her coffee parties with her two remaining friends who, like her, stayed here in the old town.

Once one had a permanent residence in Venice, the usual practical questions of everyday life about taxes, shopping options or available dentists quickly arose. Lienhard soon discovered the advantages of having his own boat and even got a driver's license for it.

As a result, Lienhard visited the same places in Venice at different times of the year, making the places more tangible for himself and also taking on a few temporary jobs in order to get closer to people and experience banalities.

First he worked in the evening in the kitchen of a restaurant near the Rialto Bridge. He then was hired for a month at a shipyard in the Dorsoduro district. Also he helped with the vegetable harvest on Sant'Erasmo and eventually worked in an antique shop in the Castello district.

In the end a whole year passed in Venice, but he noticed that he was always haunted by a kind of ambivalence. Sometimes, in the months of March, August, September, November, he felt a sense of truthfulness just as he wanted it to be. The other months everything felt unreal. The feeling came and went, with no discernible pattern.

He learned: the ideal moment is a diva.

Ever since his stay in Venice had become a timeless endeavor, he had lost the urge to own the place. Visits were in no hurry, because he would be able to see everything at any time; it was always available anyway. So he postponed some visits for later.

He had also lost the desire to photograph Venice, because everything was there. He did not need any pictures, he didn't need to take any effort for this, everything was tangible anyway. Tangible Venice.

It was enough for him to know that everything, all panoramas and views, were in good hands in Venice and had their place and that he had access to them at any time and could go to them at any time.

Everything became familiar through the tangibility.

It became trivial.

He avoided most of the public events.

The Venice Biennale in May was like a revelation for him, like a joke, because during this art exhibition, everything turned out to be not what it supposed to be. All the places that before had remained untouched by tourists, now were in fact no insider tips anymore: in every lane, no matter how remote, there was a Biennale visitor or there was an art project room.

So even the most hidden alleys were no secret anymore. Even the Castello quarter with its somewhat shabby football field, the outdated floodlights and the buildings smeared with graffiti had a charme. It was maybe the charme of evanescence, the charme of not being so smooth and beautiful like the picturesque alleys in the other quarters. Like a lost place.

But now this sloppy charme was gone with all the tourists populating the streets. Otherwise Castello would have remained a hidden pearl, Lienhard was sure of that. Maybe not really a pearl, rather an oil stain on an asphalt floor, but with a rainbow in it if one looked at it at the right angle. A place with barbs made of gold.

During the whole year in Venice, he saw a lot, got to know many people. At some point he knew every street and every canal and could claim that he knew every part of the island, because he had been very thorough. But in spite of everything, Lienhard did not know whether he had really experienced the key moment he wanted. He could not tell when Venice would come true, he was not sure if the images in his head, induced by the travel magazines, would ever be replaced by the real Venice that he now was experiencing.

When the carnival began in February, Lienhard contented himself with a short visit. It no longer bothered him to miss something. Instead, he enjoyed meeting the friends he had made here. He had got to know Carlo and his wife during his work at the shipyard some time ago. Now they invited him to their home on the first carnival weekend to eat the well-known carnival pastries: freshly made, still warm *riccioline*.

At least twice a week he went shopping at Giovanni, the local butcher, and sometimes he met his neighbor Roberto there, who always asked for a slice of sausage for his Maltese dog in his arms. The three of them chatted about the weather and Italian TV series, while in front of the small shop, so to speak in front of the waterfall, the tourists passed by and sometimes took photos of the shop from the outside. At least once a week Lienhard went to eat in Alberto's tavern, which was always hopelessly overcrowded. The patron always greeted him by his first name and patted him on the shoulder in a friendly manner.

* * *

On a hazy late afternoon in February, almost exactly a year after his arrival in Venice, Lienhard strolled through the Castello quarter, towards the harbor, as he did every day.

It was windy and the seagulls screeched as usual on the canal. A man jogged past him, followed the canal like him, punched in the air for training. This was not what a normal tourist probably would like to see. It was banal, but part of this place. It was the dark matter of Venice, so to speak. In the red house next door, as always, a woman peeked out of the skylight and watched what was happening outside. He secretly only called her "the woman who smokes" because that was exactly what she was, the woman who smokes. He actually always saw her when he walked here.

He and she nodded briefly to each other.

This was his district.

As he got closer to the harbor, he heard a strange noise and so he walked closer, stepped onto the boardwalk: the parked boats swayed in the waves, were also moved by the wind. And how these dozen, perhaps hundreds, of sail ropes hit the masts, this produced them a strange sound: bright tones like a wind chime - different pitches, bell-like, a chaotic song.

He stood there for a long time and just listened.

As soon as he walked on to the harbor quay, he made up his mind never to walk past here again in order to preserve this perfect moment forever in this mind. He would leave the canon of the boats untouched in the future, not rub off its rough charm through habit.

Even years later, he could not remember a more beautiful sound than that of the swaying lines on the boat masts, a spectacle worthy of the Art Biennale, but luckily hidden from it. Castello, this refuge, this misunderstood beauty, which he turned his back on forever after that experience reluctantly.

After this walk through the Castello district, after living in Venice for three days, five weeks and a year, he decided not only to leave Castello but also Venice, otherwise he would have had to stay there for a lifetime.

Chapter Fourteen

DURING HIS ONE-YEAR STAY IN VENICE, LIENHARD HAD RECOGNIZED
that it was not just the length of stay in one place that made him
believe he had really arrived there. It seemed to him that various
factors had an influence and he wanted to pay attention to which
conditions were particularly favorable or unfavorable for his ability
to maximally appreciate a geographic location. Therefore, he would
travel to other places until he found a conclusive explanation.

So he became a restless man who jumped from place to place for
months and even years.

Shanghai was a good example:

He arrived at Pudong International Airport early in the morning
and immediately got into a taxi to be taken to the city center. The car
drove him over a long highway bridge and he saw this city now for
the first time with his own eyes. The driver pressed the accelerator
on his old car, a Volkswagen Santana, as if he had to drive Lienhard
to an urgent appointment.

Lienhard got out of the taxi under a smog-covered sky in the
Pudong business district and looked up at the 468-meter-high Pearl
Tower, which one saw often when people talked about Shanghai.

A short time later he was upstairs, looking down from the

panorama window at the skyscrapers and streets in the distance. However, he was missing something. He thought about it, paced up and down, looked out every window, stood on the transparent glass floor and looked into the depths. It was nice here, but he didn't feel any satisfaction in being here. The place seemed interchangeable to him. He could have been in another city and in another country now. He lacked the unmistakable.

For 30 yuan, he bought a ticket for a trip through an underground sightseeing tunnel that subverted the 600-meter-wide Huangpu River and brought it to the other bank.

Later he stood on the river bank and looked back at the skyline of Pudong. He gazed at the various skyscrapers and saw the Pearl Tower from a distance. Its characteristic shape of vertically lined up giant pearls could now be seen at a glance and the tower stood out visually from the other buildings on the modern skyline.

Lienhard looked at the skyline, he compared the sight with his travel guide. Yes, now it was like the picture. The majority of the pictures he was familiar with from Shanghai were depicted exactly this section of exactly this quarter from exactly this distance. That was a good thing. This circumstance was by no means a guarantee, nevertheless the factors seemed to take effect, because Lienhard had just sensed a change.

Something happened to him.

He felt it now all of a sudden.

There it was, the desired effect: something changed, shifted, locked in place in his mind. It seemed to him that he felt an inner click, snap, because he had caught the right moment. It didn't always happen as quickly as this time. And it didn't always happen at all. But that was the only effect that counted for him.

Perfect, so he was actually in Shanghai now, it was really true. Now everything finally came together. It felt real, like a perfect moment. That was exactly what he was looking for. Yes, that was all right, he was presented with exactly the sight that he had wanted to see and that right now gave him everything he wanted. A precision landing.

For a while he just stood there and let the scenery take effect. Maybe half an hour or more went by. This city, this address, this place, which just a few hours ago he had somehow considered to be unreal, only a picture, had now become real.

Lienhard was very satisfied and also surprised how quickly it worked this time. The mission had been accomplished now. Once more he looked from the Bund at the Pearl Tower, consciously perceived the noises around him, yes, he perceived everything: the flowing water, the distant traffic, the honking of the countless mopeds, the conversations of the businessmen on the phone.

He enjoyed the pause for minutes.

At one point he checked his watch and made a few calls to make changes to his schedule.

It was now ten o'clock in the morning and he had been in Shanghai for almost three hours. He took a taxi to the airport and then sat down in the waiting room with a sandwich and a drink to wait for boarding, which would start in four hours.

Tokyo was waiting.

Chapter Fifteen

THERE WERE 195 STATES, THOUSANDS OF CITIES, AND AN ALMOST infinite number of travel destinations worldwide. The number of trips forced Lienhard to proceed as efficiently as possible, to plan the trips carefully.

A few months earlier he had worked through the African continent selectively (Table Mountain in Cape Town, Johannesburg, Cape of Good Hope, coffee plantation in Ethiopia plus coffee ceremony with popcorn, Robben Island, safari through the Kruger National Park, Serengeti).

He had also dealt with Pakistan, Mongolia, Russia, Vietnam and India within a short time. One pending topic that he was looking forward to was Australia.

Currently, it was no longer just a matter of working through his list from the *Brockhaus*.

He was looking for that particular moment when he really enjoyed to visit a travel destination. In the meantime, Lienhard had compiled various reasons that he believed had an influence. He called them *travel hypotheses*.

· · ·

Travel hypothesis No. 1. Marginal utility: Lienhard believed that a lot had to do with the length of stay and the economic principle of marginal utility. The higher the consumption of a product, the greater the benefit, but at some point one was saturated and the benefits reached their limits, sooner or later - like while travelling a country or a certain travel destination.

Travel hypothesis no. 2. Recognition: When traveling, Lienhard seemed to be looking for what he already knew, a sign of recognition that showed him that he was really in the right place. However, it also could happen the opposite. Sometimes he also enjoyed a place that offered something atypical, unexpected, regardless of what he was actually looking for.

Travel hypothesis No. 3. Emergence: Sometimes it seemed to Lienhard, that he did not see the forest for the trees and the comparison with the own expectation didn't work. The place was more than the sum of its parts and so it became harder to know when Lienhard had seen enough of that place.

Travel hypothesis No. 4. Abstraction: For Lienhard, a place he visited was initially Terra Incognita and the name of the place meant nothing, it was an empty phrase: London. Istanbul. Sahara Desert. Before he was there himself, everything remained an abstraction, but afterwards it didn't necessarily become more believable. Often he was unable to reconcile the imaginary object with the real object, perhaps because he was overwhelmed with the object in front of his eyes and everything was still saved as an abstraction.

Travel hypothesis no. 5. Habit: At first, a place was something iconic for Lienhard, simply because it represented a worthwhile goal for him, which he had now achieved. But then Lienhard often quickly got used to it, and the nimbus of the unattainable and legendary peeled off. Something tangible and banal emerged and boredom occured.

There were probably other possible explanations why Lienhard was in some cases happy about a successful sighting and sometimes not. He got the impression that these travel hypotheses helped him understand the problem, but not to solve it, because even if he knew about these restrictions and conditions, he could not influence his travel experience.

Chapter Sixteen

It wasn't as hot as July and August, but it was already oppressive.

His hotel was in a neighborhood near the main train station.

Tired of his many travels, Lienhard had decided to take things a little easier for Spain. He would just stroll randomly through the city as if he were a normal tourist and not someone who was looking for something very specific.

A friendly man spoke to him.

Whether he wanted tickets for the city tour with the red bus for fifteen euros.

Lienhard chose a window seat on the upper floor. It smelled of gummy bears. Three young Britons to his left, about twenty years old, were having a great time, holding their cans of energy drinks casually with just three fingers.

Lienhard put the headphones in his ear and switched to channel four (German). The tape with the tourist information was aged, but it taught him tourist wisdom about the city's history.

A friendly Japanese man sat next to him for a few stops, marking the attractions on his city map that were just being explained. The buildings they passed were reflected in his thick glasses. Then at some point the Japanese got out at a plaza and Lienhard never saw him again.

In the afternoon Lienhard sat on a concrete bollard in a shady place in the Triana district, watching a small group of pensioners on the other side of the street, sitting on their balconies.

He observed how they were taking their drinks or reading a book —

They were waiting for something —

He looked at them for a while. Later, when he looked into the distance, he discovered the roof garden of a skyscraper diagonally opposite. The laundry patiently dried up in the mild Seville wind.

An old cat was curled up asleep right next to his feet. He looked at her for a while, saw her breathing calmly, thought it was nice to have a small, furry being by his side.

Only over time did he perceive the scent that he had been inhaling the whole time in the tree shade. The orange trees were in bloom above him.

At some point around 5 p.m. he was walking as a lone wolf along the Rio Guadalquivir. A group of young anglers waited on the other bank for a catch. That certain smell wafted towards him from the water, that cozy grouch that rivers sometimes brought with them.

A flock of birds in V formation passed across the river.

The sky was now very cloudy.

On the ground an empty Fanta can rolled in the wind.

Lienhard felt lost in this place, but it really didn't matter where he was. He was lost everywhere.

Later, Lienhard sat on the upper deck of a tourist boat, surrounded by green plastic chairs. The rain pelted on the plastic sheeting above him. Over on the bank: the monastery in which Columbus had lived. Several people waved to from the bank, perhaps the anglers from earlier, and he felt compelled to wave back as he was the only person on deck.

* * *

In the evening he went to the nearby so-called *Carboneria*, the truism of initiated tourists. An insider tip that his *Merian live*-Travellers-Guide also had to offer.

In these old walls, in which coal was once stored, nowadays "legendary flamenco performances" took place according to the description of the travel guide.

First he drank an *Agua de Sevilla*, a tasty delicacy made from pineapple juice, cava wine, whiskey, Cointreau and ice, garnished with whipped cream and cinnamon. Then he asked for tapas: four pieces of Manchego cheese and four half, but thick slices of salami were carefully draped on an A4 sheet of paper and some snacks were placed next to them.

To be there: to see more than the travel guide has to say and instead to see things directly in detail, to see unimportant details, yes, he loved that, it gave him the feeling of really being here, in the middle of the action, being part of the iconic place.

The flamenco singer was young, but his voice was deep and old. The dancing lady, tall, robust, powerful, tapped energetically and with chattering teeth to the beat of the music.

Lienhard was very happy with Seville.

His Sevilla-travel-gain so far has been good.

When Lienhard happened to look at the table next door, he winced. In the vague twilight he saw a woman he knew.

Ms. Reber.

He and Ms. Reber met by chance in Mumbai six months ago. That day they had strolled through town together for hours, visiting the markets overflowing with goods and people.

Then something happened.

An incident full of agape.

It was about an Indian family.

There happened a moment of light.

Lienhard had never told anyone about it, as any description would only have banalized everything. In a nutshell, it was the goodness of one person, yes, of this person sitting next to him, that had impressed him so much. Afterwards, they had sat together in the taxi and drove through the night of Mumbay. Mrs. Reber had looked out the window into the night and only said: "It's nice, somehow, out there, the lights of the sleeping city." So they had silently watched the lights of the sleeping city through the car window until they finally reached the hotel. But more than the lights of the city, he had kept looking at the shadow beside him, that precious sight of a silhouette that he was slowly beginning to love.

And so now they both happened to be sitting here in a Spanish Flamenco house just by coincidence.

Later, after the last flamenco performance, he accompanied her to the nearest taxi station. Lienhard had a flight in two hours and Ms. Reber had to go back to her hotel. So they agreed to see each other again in Paris in the fall.

Their two cars continued in the opposite direction and from his moving taxi, Lienhard gazed after her taxi in the rearview mirror until it finally turned at the end of the street and disappeared behind a building.

Chapter Seventeen

He began his two-day stay in Madrid at five in the morning in an grumpy mood.

The city could have been made of pure gold and he would have hated it in that first moment. Because he had been reluctant to take this domestic flight in the early hours of the morning after meeting Mrs. Reber by chance. But now he was here without her.

In Madrid, Lienhard did his planned sightings. One day before leaving for Barcelona, he learned that his flight would be canceled. He booked a regional train instead.

After the many flights in his life, it was strange to suddenly be on the ground while traveling. He would really have to earn Barcelona.

On a four-hour journey in a non-air-conditioned wagon, the train plowed its way inland to Saragossa and then worked its way back towards the coast for another four hours. A train station for a god, he thought as his train pulled into Tarragona. Behind the rails and the undulating windbreak wall, ocean liners and tankers could be seen cruising the sea.

For the first time, Lienhard really looked at the people who were traveling. He saw their relaxed faces. They knew the way. Obviously, it wasn't their first time in this train. They knew what was coming. But he stayed tuned.

When the train continued towards Barcelona, sandy beaches suddenly spread to its right and there were tall palm trees like on a Caribbean island. He was gazing at the beach and the bathers. The train was approaching the coastline and suddenly it seemed to Lienhard that he was no longer an onlooker who was gliding over the rails at the foot of the beach but directly at the lido, no, even in the sea.

It looked like this as the train was at most 2 meters away from the water. Lienhard thought, that the waves of the Mediterranean sea had to reach the train. The splashes or at least the spray would reach the window. It looked surreal.

A passerby noticed Lienhard's astonishment and said in Catalan: You are probably seeing it for the first time. He just replied: yes, indeed.

* * *

After arriving in the city, he spent most of the day in the nearby Ozeaneum, seeing rays, sharks, whales and moray eels, among other things, which appealed to him very much as he had never seen any of these animals with his own eyes before.

The following early morning he went directly to the port.

The smell of fried food was in the air.

At the Cap a fair.

Small stalls with ice cream and still hot churros with chocolate sauce.

He went to the tourist bus stop there to take a round trip.

Also the next day, he walked through the city, but it seemed strange to walk the same route that he had made the day before in the cozy bus. Without any taped voice telling him where to look at, it was like something was missing.

There was just the trivial sound of the city such as cars and some hammering and milling from a construction site nearby.

Every ten minutes he met one of these tourist buses that he had used before, but now Lienhard did not belong to it anymore. Instead, for him there was now tourism for advanced so to speak. Another bus appeared. Lienhard watched the people on the upper deck as they looked around because the tape voice told them so. Lienhard felt a little envy of their journey that was so shallow and well-guarded.

Finally came April 23rd, Book and Rose Day. The custom of this festival was that women would give a book to the men they loved, and the men would give them flowers in turn. Lienhard looked at the market stalls and just let himself be carried away by the crowd, eventually reaching a side street.

He bought a folded rose made of rose-colored paper at a small stall owned by an association for the arts of origami. The rose was small and had almost no weight. He put it carefully in his jacket pocket.

Chapter Eighteen

In September of the same year, after various other trips, he
finally flew to Paris and met Ms. Reber there. Together they
followed an avenue of plane trees along the Seine.

Sometimes they would stop to look at the antiquarian books and
prints that were on display in the *boîtes*. These were historical
wooden market stalls looking like green boxes. Their roof could be
folded down.

Along the sidewalk, dozens of them were lined up. Most of the
sellers had their books, which were neatly sorted by author, wrapped
in transparent cellophane and handwritten on the edge with the
author's name: MOLIERE, BEAUVOIR, SARTRE.

Finally Ms. Reber found a small red book by Albert Camus at a
stand and she bought it for 5 euros from the *bouquinist*, a friendly,
older man in his seventies.

Later they talked about his travels and Mrs. Reber asked him
about a special travel experience.

He thought about it and then said: "From all my travels I often
think back to Crete: to Heraklion and the street dogs there. On the
eve of my onward journey to Madagascar, I sat next to the old port,
in the middle of the wasteland, and looked at the sea. The sun had

already disappeared behind the horizon and the towers of the raki distilleries were already shining in the distance. I felt out of place, not there, not in Greece, but without purpose, no matter where I was. Then I looked at the sea and watched the waves break on the cast concrete blocks on the shore. In that moment I hated to know more about the different types of breakwater blocks - dolosse, tetrapod, quadripod - than about a fulfilled love. But I knew that I would always have a crazy view of everything, no matter what I would ever do, because I would always be a stranger to the world because of my story. Then, a five-headed, colorfully mixed group of street dogs approached me, three small and three large ones, and they sat a few meters next to me in the sand. The nearest one was their pack leader, a beautiful white, somewhat dusty shepherd dog. They just sat there and kept me company. "

Ms. Reber said nothing, but as they walked on, she hooked her arm on him. When they crossed the bridge, a car stopped at the pedestrian crosswalk and let them pass. It was so sunny and warm that autumn day in Paris that at this moment he even smelled the strange smell of the heated air that radiated from the sheet metal of the hood. It was a ridiculous detail that probably nobody before had ever thought about, but he noticed it because every second was remarkable now.

He looked at the old walls of Notre-Dame. How many cohorts had already been smashed by the timelessness of this wall? This wall had seen many lifes come and go. There was no gloating about the losses, but there was the equanimity of a giant.

Lienhard sensed her arm around his arm, and for a moment he felt like something indestructible, eternal, that could survive even this old building at the side of a loved one.

Because they were here, beautiful, alive, present. The cemeteries seemed to him something anachronistic, a verdict that had long since been repealed. Because the world surrounded them both and it was absurd to assume that anything could ever change about that. Wasn't it absurd that a thinking, loving mind could ever succumb to absence?

Later he gave her the origami rose. She wrote something in Camus' red book and promised Lienhard to bring it to him at their next meeting.

But things turned out differently.

A few weeks later, Ms. Reber wrote to him that her ex-husband had desperately asked her to travel with him to India as a humanitarian worker to help those in need there. Lienhard sighed, but recognized the greatness of the two and let Ms. Reber go.

Chapter Nineteen

ONE DAY LIENHARD DECIDED THAT HE HAD TRAVELED ENOUGH AND that his *Brockhaus* list had also been sufficiently processed. In any case, he had enough of his unsteady life and wanted to have a normal everyday life again.

So he found a job at a bank, quickly worked his way up and eventually became a financial auditor. His life was regular and smooth again and he began to settle down. Months and years passed, but he never forgot Ms. Reber.

* * *

Then, on an ordinary afternoon, when he came home from a walk, it happened. That afternoon he climbed the linoleum-covered wooden staircase to his old apartment on the third floor, as he did every day, and on the second floor he saw an empty chewing gum wrap lying on a stair step. It was lying on the well-worn step that was quite dents in the middle.

The silver wrapping was lying there slightly crumpled up. It was torn and it read "*Mint extra strong*" on it.

And it was funny: this little gum wrapper pleased him as much as this old stairwell.

Because he suddenly thought: welcome home.

He didn't mean his apartment or the stairwell but all stairwells in the world: they were so wonderfully normal. Because this chewing gum wrap was lying there casually and nobody worried about it. There were millions of other chewing gum wrap that lay somewhere and no one cared about them. They quietly attested that casualness of the world which he had lacked for so long.

<h1 style="text-align: center;">Chapter Twenty</h1>

Walser gazed at the small safe on the kitchen table.

So that was it now.

Pandora's box, so to speak.

He was worried by Lienhard's hint that people had died for the information in it, and he wondered if it was even advisable to know the secret. Maybe he should go while he could. He had urged Lienhard to tell him his secret, but now he didn't want to rush anything.

First he had to find out more about Lienhard and understand in which direction this was all going.

Nobody knew what effects the assassination attempt had on Lienhard. Perhaps he had psychological problems since then and was no longer sane. Ultimately, Lienhard lived here in the caravan like a hermit or dropout. Loneliness could do a lot to a person.

"Before you show me any evidence now, I would like to understand where you found the flat earth. How did you come up with it? You don't spontaneously decide to completely change your world view, I guess", said Walser.

"It was when I was traveling to the Aegean. Then everything changed", said Lienhard.

Walser was disappointed.

He had hoped Lienhard would tell him a great story about Antarctica and the edge of the world that he had found. It was not that he believed in that rubbish, but at least it would have been an entertaining narrative. Instead, Lienhard was about to drop a fairy tale about the Mediterranean. It would be almost too easy to refute Lienhard.

"What's got the Aegean to do with it? I just can imagine that you will tell me that you have been in Greece and from there you saw Atlas carrying the firmament on his back", said Walser and laughed.

"No, I was in Turkey. I saw a total solar eclipse from there. Then, I understood the flat earth", replied Lienhard.

"I still don't understand how this is connected. In a solar eclipse, the sun is covered by the moon. So what? If instead you would have told me about a lunar eclipse, then it would have made more sense to me. For example if you would have told me that during a lunar eclipse, there had been a disc-shaped shadow of the earth on the moon. Then you could convince me, but –"

"It's not that simple!" Lienhard interrupted him. He looked more irritable than at the Flat Earthers Congress.

„In fact, it's very simple", said Walser, „the flat earth is a fairy tale. Either you are kidding your followers willfully or you actually believe this garbage. I don't know which is worse."

Walser was sure that now he could win the battle. He only had to provoke him further. Then Lienhard would confess something accidently.

"The flat earth theory is not a fairy tale!" said Lienhard in a loud voice, „in fact, the globe is the actual fairytale!" Then he put his coffee cup on the table with a loud bang.

Then he fell silent and seemed to be thinking.

Walser waited for an explanation from Lienhard, but Lienhard fell into stubborn silence after he broke out, stirring the full coffee cup with the spoon, lost in thought.

Walser had not expected this reaction. He knew that Lienhard could be an energetic interlocutor who represented the concerns of the Flat Earther better than anyone else. But at the moment he didn't seem to be aggressive, instead he looked rather sullen. Perhaps the tiger had lost its teeth after the bomb attack.

Walser tore open a sugar bag and let trickle down the granulated sugar into his cup.

What was he doing here?

The two men sat across from each other at the small kitchen table without saying a word, sipping their cups of steaming coffee. It was too quiet in the trailer.

Only the drizzle outside was dripping audibly onto the roof, which at least was pleasantly calming.

But the situation wasn't quite that harmless. Walser was suspicious of Lienhard because he knew that there were terrible accusations against Lienhard.

There were bad incidents regarding Lienhard and the Flat Earthers. Walser knew that shortly before the Flat Earthers Congress there had taken place an murder investigation. Hans Meier had been assassinated. He was a famous physicist and astronomer.

Meier had probably been the most vehement critic of the Flat Earthers ever. Now he was dead.

During his investigations before the flat earth congress, Walser had found out a very explosive secret: there had been a meeting between Lienhard and Meier shortly before his death.

It had never been made public what it was about, but Lienhard had never been charged, although he was the focus of murder investigators. Allegedly the file was kept under lock and key at the highest level and the case was filed as a "cold case".

Lienhard was influential and had a lot of money. Maybe he had bought himself out. On the other hand, Lienhard had received threats again and again in the past and he was also protected by bodyguards at the congress at the time. If one could believe some reports, several employees of Lienhard, who worked in different observatories in Chile, had fatal accidents. It seemed life-threatening to know Lienhard.

A beep broke the silence. Lienhard pressed a button on his watch and got up resolutely. He turned to the sink and picked up a plastic box lying in the cupboard below. Then he pulled out an old cheap cell phone and inserted a brand new SIM card into the device. Less than half a minute later, he received a text message.

Without a word he left the trailer, closed the door behind him and called someone on the cell phone.

Walser watched him through the window, but couldn't hear much.

Lienhard spoke English and Spanish, but Walser caught the fact that Lienhard asked his interlocutor to go into hiding and go to safety. Lienhard also said something about "unclear situation... "...maybe too late... ", "...time-window..." and "...don't trust anyone...", but also" ... eliminate..." and "...when it's all over...". Then he immediately switched off the cell phone and removed the SIM card.

Walser thought of Meier's harsh criticism of Lienhard and of his sudden end. He wondered if it had been wise to meet Lienhard alone and in such a remote place. Of course it wasn't, but he wanted to know more about this strange Flat Earthers case. However, Walser became more and more suspicious of Lienhard's behaviour. This crazy man presumably considered him an enemy too, having written several negative newspaper articles about the Flat Earthers. Perhaps now Lienhard would take revenge.

Sure, Walser had left a note in his apartment this morning, but that would no longer be of any use to him personally. If something happened to him, it wouldn't be comforting to know that his killer would be caught later.

Lienhard came back into the trailer and appeared to be nervous but he had dropped his silence.

"What are you thinking of?" asked Lienhard.

"I am thinking of Meier. Nobody knows what happened to him. Only his murderer knows", said Walser.

"Yes, a tragic loss," said Lienhard.

"You saw him before he died", said Walser.

"Yes, indeed", replied Lienhard, „we talked to each other."

"Police found out that he was poisoned", said Walser

"Yes, I heard that too. Said to have been a slow-acting poison", said Lienhard with a strange expression on his face.

"He was your archenemy–", said Walser. Lienhard was gazing at him in a strange way.

"We hated each other before we met", said Lienhard, confirming Walser's fears.

"And after that? You were interrogated by the police after Meier's death", said Walser.

"That's true. But the case has since been shelved by the authorities. It was never officially cleared up. A cold case", said Lienhard, playing with the empty sugar wrap that Walser previously had emptied for his coffee.

"So the killer is still free", concluded Walser.

"Yes, probably you are right. But I think this will all soon come to an end", said Lienhard and crumpled up the paper in his hand.

"As far as I know, you were one of the last people who saw Meier alive", Walser said. He didn't want to further provoke Lienhard, but he had to find out if he was safe here.

"Yes, maybe I was the last person he spoke to", said Lienhard.

"How could you convince the police of not being guilty?" asked Walser.

"Actually, I couldn't convince the police", said Lienhard, „after the attack, I had to go into hiding. Not even the police knows where I am. You are the first person apart from my closes confidantes who knows it."

Lienhard didn't seem to notice that he was arousing more and more Walser's suspicions. Or maybe he just didn't care. Maybe for a good reason. Ten years from now, hikers might accidentally make a strange discovery in the forest here. The finally cleared up "Missing Walser case".

Walser was unsettled.

Walser looked at his empty coffee cup, observed the dark edges that the drink had left. A few of the sugar crystals did not appear to have dissolved. He poked at it with the coffee spoon, paying attention to the crunch, and wasn't sure how normal sugar crystals crunched.

"Would you like another coffee?" asked Lienhard.

"No thanks," said Walser. He tried to remember the taste of the coffee, the aftertaste, tried to find out whether there was something unusual.

Again they sat opposite each other in silence. For the first time since he was here, Walser found the silence threatening. Walser wondered if he was sitting across from a weirdo or maybe even a murderer.

Anyone who believed in a flat earth had to be expected to do crazy things.

Chapter Twenty-One

Three months before the bomb attac, Max Lienhard was extremely satisfied. He had just returned from an international Flat Earthers congress in Texas and the event had far exceeded all of his expectations.

Things were going well for the Flat Earthers right now.

Together with two helpers, Lienhard processed the third batch of today's "fan letters".

He carefully pulled a letter at random from the pile. Basically, he had nothing to fear, at least not physically, because specialists checked all mail for explosives and CBRN-hazards beforehand.

With the exception of around 250 mailings, all of today's letters were harmless.

So today was a good day.

The first letter was handwritten and came from Italy: *Thank you for opening my eyes, because our governments are lying to us about the true shape of the earth. Eventually everything will be revealed.*

The second letter had no return address and was written on the computer: *Dear fools, please stop this madness! Yesterday, my son told me that he had read on the Internet that the earth was flat. Since then, he thinks that his geography teacher is lying. It is because of you that our children go stupid!*

The letter was put on today's "Haters" pile, as was the next letter (*Stop this idiocy. They have no idea about astronomy. You weirdo!*).

Also the next letter had to be placed on that pile as it contained bad insults.

A striking number of teachers wrote to him.

They complained that their students were rebellious.

They said, there is a riot in their class rooms.

Max Lienhard laughed out loud. He was just reading a letter from two Flat Earth fans. Even Lienhard thought that they were dumbasses. The two men had written to him that they were ready to sacrifice themselves as martyrs for the Flat Earther idea. They would shortly be filmed during their kamikaze mission. Their plan was to drive a snowmobile to the edge of the earth's disk and then plunge into space during a live broadcast.

Lienhard put a few more letters on the third pile: "Threats". His life was pretty dangerous. The good thing about it was that at the same time, he supported the Flat Earth project. As long as his statements polarized, he had the public's attention. His aim was to get as much attention as possible. That's why he made sure that the Flat Earthers were constantly providing some updates about their activities to the public. Among other things, he collected signatures for the fact that schools and universities should alternatively teach the possibility of a flat earth. There were also TV spots with several internationally known celebrities who explained why they believed in a flat earth.

Various teachers' associations and scientists fought for a ban on the Flat Earther publications, which Lienhard was very accommodating. They made his organization better known.

There was only one downer for him: Various physicists at CERN in Geneva published a manifesto in various daily newspapers in which they attacked Lienhard directly. They wrote that the ancient flat earth idea was an *assault on today's enlightened society and science.*

They stated, that one had to fight Lienhard's heresy by all means. So they also were fighting against his recently founded "Professorship for the Exploration of the Flat Earth" at a German University. The manifesto ended with the words: *We must not leave teaching and research to amateurs like Max Lienhard and other conspiracy theorists.*

On the one hand, this manifesto was very good for the Flat Earthers. It showed that the awareness for the flat earth theory was increasing. On the other hand, Lienhard had seen that besides the other signatures of the manifesto, there was also the name of Ms. Reber who actually was a former CERN physicist. Today, she still was in India on her humanitarian aid project and the fact that she had taken the effort to protest against him and his organization was painful for him.

After that, he emailed her and she agreed to meet him when she would be in Spain that year.

Chapter Twenty-Two

Lienhard first noticed it three weeks before the bomb attack on the Flat Earthers Congress. It was Sunday evening when he got home from the Flat Earthers headquarters.

He happened to look out the window of his apartment on the third floor and saw a black SUV, which was about 400 meters away in the private parking lot across the street.

Lienhard knew that something was wrong, because the 75-year-old Mrs. Greta Sattler, who owned this parking lot but didn't own a car, usually guarded it doggedly. She had inherited it from her husband Albert, a former car chauffeur. So she always kept an eye on the parking lot, even fencing it with a massive chain so that no outsiders could park there. It was strange that her parking lot now was occupied.

At first, Lienhard feared that something had happened to the lady. Maybe she had been injured in the apartment.

However, Mrs. Sattler seemed to be doing well. Lienhard just saw her go out of the house to buy her rolls from the bakery nextdoor. The strange car was still there. Mrs. Sattler walked past the car very quickly, as it seemed to Lienhard, but she did not look at the car, as if she were afraid of paying too much attention to the car. The car windows were tinted, so Lienhard couldn't tell whether someone was sitting in it. A few hours later the parking lot was free again. But in the evening Lienhard noticed the same car again.

There could be many reasons why such a car was parked here. Maybe it had nothing to do with Lienhard. What was strange, however, was that his telephone line was rustling recently, as if someone was listening to him. But it could be that he just was paranoid.

Actually, the threatening letters had decreased, but there were more physical attacks against his organization.

Somebody had thrown raw eggs against the facade of his house. The website of his organization had been hacked and Globe Earthers had published the famous Blue Marble picture with the words *Flat Earthers, let yourself be shot at the moon!* Two days ago, a group called *Globe Truth* had broken into the Flat Earthers headquarter and had stolen a huge bronze sculpture of the disk-shaped earth. In addition, they had nailed a poster on the entrance door of the Flat Earthers headquarters with the title: *Manifesto of the true spherical shape of the world.* There were listed 100 reasons why the earth was a sphere.

Lienhard's cell phone rang.

"This is Hans Meier speaking, we have to talk", the man on the phone greeted him straightforwardly in an almost military tone.

Meier was a world-class astronomer. A comet was named after the 63-year-old Swiss and he had also discovered an exoplanet in another solar system six months ago. Meier's achievements in astronomy were great and the most important universities around the world repeatedly asked him for lectures. The city of Zurich even gave him an honorary office in the *Urania observatory*. Meier loved the stars. And Meier hated the Flat Earthers. He would do anything to fight them.

"Nice to hear from you. But what exactly do we need to talk about?" asked Lienhard.

"I think you know that very well. I have been leaked explosive information about you, which should be of interest to the public. I would like to hear from you whether this allegation is true. Afterwards, I will decide whether this should become an issue in the media", said Meier in an angry voice.

"What exactly do you mean?"asked Lienhard.

"We have to meet," said Meier.

Lienhard did not go any further into Meier's vague allusions. He was convinced that Meier didn't know anything and was only bluffing to watch Lienhard's reaction.

It was true, however: Lienhard actually had an explosive secret from the past. By all means, he would prevent Meier from disclosing it to the public.

One of his secrets was that he was working on a confidential project in South America and the Antarctic. He had put together a small, powerful team. They were his closest confidantes: José, Rodrigo and Pavel, all three of them highly intelligent and absolutely loyal, who worked for him in secret and who had rented a small observatory on the plateau of Chile. His second team was in the Antarctic.

Neither the public nor his Flat Earthers colleagues knew about it, but he would reveal everything at the congress in Lucerne and then cause a sensation.

On the phone he now cleverly avoided Meier's questions. Still, it was clear to him that a meeting was inevitable. At least he would have to check the level of knowledge of his adversary. It was important to listen to Meier before he could take the adequate measures. He would meet him after the Flat Earthers Congress.

Basically, Lienhard did not have an aversion to Meier. Actually, he even admired him. Meier initially worked for a few years as a math and physics teacher at a grammar school in order to get young people excited about the knowledge.

He later returned to the Faculty of Astronomy to devote himself entirely to space exploration. He did not correspond to the cliché of an unworldly researcher with corduroy pants and shaggy hair, who looked for spiral fog at night and had nothing else in life than his math calculations. Meier was a tanned, handsome man with blond-silver hair and a sporty stature. He was a hedonist and athlete who, in addition to numbers and stars, also valued a good wine under the blue sky of the Costa Brava.

Lienhard was intellectually equal, but so far there had been no direct confrontation. He arranged an early meeting with Meier. Then he would find out how much his adversary actually knew.

Chapter Twenty-Three

Two days before the big Flat Earthers Congress in Lucerne, in the early afternoon, Lienhard left the Flat Earthers office on *Bellevue Square* in Zurich and went to the tram.

He loved this tram station, which was covered with a huge, flat disk. It reminded him of the model of a flat earth.

When he looked up, he saw a graffiti in thick black letters: *The Globe model sucks!*

It seemed that slowly the idea was diffunding within society. The current change was felt everywhere. The Flat Earther base grew steadily while the Globe Earthers lost support.

It was important that he would channel the movement, especially in the next few months. He wanted to avoid violence. But actually it already took place from time to time.

Two days ago, a book burning had taken place in a quarry near Zurich. The crowd had created a pyre and then piled all objects that stood for the globe: astronomy books, atlases, NASA pictures, terrestrial photos, space DVDs, world maps and planet posters. On top, they stacked hundreds of globes. The fire had been visible for miles.

But the Globe Earthers weren't reluctant either.

One group had beat up a well-known Flat Earther. The servers of the private University where Lienhard had his professorship were hacked. Like the Flat Earthers, the Globe Earthers were basically a very heterogeneous group.

Some Globe Earthers were enthusiastic astronomers like Meier, who looked at the night sky with the telescope and regularly sent the city administration letters of complaint about light pollution.

Other Globe Earthers were in reality quite indifferent and were not very interested in what happened outside of the earth or even outside of their village. The Flat Earthers were ahead of these people. They were not indifferent, because after all, it was a burden to reveal themselves as Flat Earther.

He got on the tram and sat down next to a teenager who looked at him and said: "I know you from television. You are the Flat Earthers boss. My classmates laugh at me because of you. They all believe in flat earth. Now I am the outsider. It's all because of you!"

Lienhard discovered an article in the daily newspaper that he didn't like at all. An investigative journalist wrote about his alleged secret project. The author did not know the exact details, but he had located the observatory in Chile, which Lienhard rented and where his team was working.

Chapter Twenty-Four

When he got home, Lienhard received a call from José. He expected that José would complain because of the newspaper article that mentioned their work in the observatory. But José had other problems.

He told Lienhard that during their preparations for Lienhard's secret project, they had discovered something stunning. José spoke quickly and erratically and kept switching from English to Spanish, repeatedly shouting "gigante descubrimiento!", a great discovery! He should calm down, said Lienhard. But José was too excited.

Now Rodrigo could be heard talking to José soothingly and finally taking the phone. Lienhard also recognized excitement in Rodrigo's voice. But he did not want to specify on the phone what they had discovered.

There were still more clarifications to be made, he said. He also mentioned that the implications were still unclear. Rodrigo asked whether the phone line was secure. Lienhard said: maybe not. So he asked Rodrigo to send him the data in encrypted form so that he could later view the information himself.

In the distance he heard car doors slamming. Lienhard happened to looked out the window through the blinds. The black SUV was back in the parking lot. Maybe the investigative journalist, who had written the article about Lienhard's secret project, was now observing him.

Rodrigo sent him a download link via an encrypted email. Apparently it was a larger, extensive document.

Lienhard heard some voices. Several men were talking. He instinctively turned off the light in his study and went back to the window to see.

For the first time, Lienhard saw who was using the SUV. Three well-dressed men stood by the car. They didn't look like Globe Earthers who planned to throw eggs at his window.

The men now stood directly under the lantern. The first one obviously checked his tablet. The second phoned and pointed to the apartment building in which Lienhard lived. The third was holding something. It looked like a gun with silencer.

Then the men marched in his direction. He had a maximum of two or three minutes to get out of here. It seemed obvious that they planned to kidnap or kill him.

Rodrigo called again. Lienhard did not answer. First he had to secure the received data from Chile and take it with him. The men weren't allowed to find it on his PC. They weren't allowed to find him either.

He inserted a USB stick into the desktop computer and started the download, while in the pale blue light of the computer screen he gathered up the essentials and packed them into his sports backpack, along with his cell phone, wallet and car keys.

The download was 73 percent complete.

Rodrigo called again. Out of an impulse, he took the call. He learned that his team had just left the observatory and now they were apparently driving downhill in Jose's car.

Rodrigo said that previously, they had been forced to leave the building. Some alleged employees of the local energy company had entered the observatory and asked them to immediately stop their work. They were told that there was a dangerous problem with a gas pipe in the basement of the observatory. When José replied that the building did not have any gas pipelines, the intruders became rude and maneuvered Lienhard's team out of the building.

Lienhard looked at the computer screen. Download progress: 89 percent.

The three astronomers had only been able to take their notebooks and some documents with them, but a lot was left behind in the observatory. Lienhard couldn't understand every word because the telephone connection was bad. There were a number of dead zones in the wasteland of the Chilean desert.

"We are being followed!" he heard José shout.

Then there was a loud bang.

Lienhard's three friends shouted loudly.

Suddenly the connection was broken.

Lienhard stood there for a moment as if paralyzed. Then he tried to focus again. There was nothing he could do for his friends now, except to move the data to a safe place and to inform the police in Chile. He had to get out of the flat immediately.

95 percent.

He thought he could hear the SUV guys downstairs in front of the main entrance to the apartment building. There was no longer any chance of leaving the apartment via the stairwell. Nevertheless, he opened the front door to give the impression that he had made the hasty escape this way.

The download was complete.

He grabbed the USB stick and ran to the kitchen, which led directly to the balcony on the courtyard side. The balcony door could be blocked from outside. It was about three meters from up here to the floor of the green inner courtyard.

He climbed over the balcony railing and shimmy to the lowest part, which he could hold on to. His feet dangled over the ground.

When he heard the voices approaching, he dropped to the floor. The lawn was soft and the landing was relatively gentle. In the dark he grope around through the spacious courtyard, which housed many shrubs and deciduous trees that completely obscured the view from above. He only looked up briefly at his apartment. There was now light in his office and shadows were moving.

He finally reached an exit via four other gardens in the large inner courtyard. Then he went to his car. Nobody seemed to be following him and he left the village quickly.

Lienhard drove a few kilometers until he reached a forest. He parked his car on a forest path by the road and turned off all the lights. Only the crescent moon shone. Otherwise it was pitch black.

He turned on his cell phone. Rodrigo hadn't tried to call him again. Probably Lienhard's cell phone was tapped or someone would try to locate it, but he had to warn his second team that was situated in Antarctica. He texted their satellite phone with a few cryptic sentences that only his team could understand. They would know what to do.

He had probably already been monitored for the past few weeks and months. Everybody who was in contact with him was in danger, including Ms. Reber. He wrote her a short email warning her.

He knew that he had to let the congress take place anyway. He did not know what data his team had discovered tough. But he was on a mission. His project was nearly finalized and he would reveal it on the congress.

After calling the police, he switched off his cell phone, smashed all the important parts with a stone and buried everything in the damp soil at the edge of the forest. Lienhard was still in shock, but he had to be focussed and efficient now. He knew who could help him now.

He drove off immediately.

Chapter Twenty-Five

It was now almost midnight, but when Lienhard looked up at the building, he saw light in one of the upper windows, directly under the dome. Someone was still working in the tower in the *Urania* star observatory in Zurich, most likely Hans Meier.

He was also in danger, because presumably all people who had contact with Lienhard in the past few weeks were systematically wiretapped. But Lienhard needed his help now.

When he rang the doorbell, he was immedialy allowed to enter. Meier met him right at the elevator exit in front of his office. He looked amazed but calm.

Probably he had been doing calculations and looking through the telescope for many hours.

"Come in", was all he said.

There was a smell of coffee in his small office. Lienhard looked through one of the small windows. From here you had a nice view of the city lights.

Lienhard explained his situation to him and put the data stick on the desk. Meier nodded. He still loathed the Flat Earthers and was annoyed at how successfully Lienhard had built them up over the years, but he immediately understood how critical the situation was.

Lienhard still owed him an explanation about all the Flat Earthers crap. Have your colleagues in Chile proven the flat earth after all and is NASA after you? Such a remark was in his mind, but he did not say a word. Instead, Meier listened to what Lienhard had to tell him. He opened the pizzabox.

"Would you also like to have a slice?" Meier asked. The night delivery service had brought him the pizza right a few minutes before Lienhard rang the doorbell.

"No, there is no time for that, I am not hungry anyway, I have to tell you everything exactly now", Lienhard just said and went on talking.

Meier listened to him while eating the Pizza which still was quite hot.

Meier let Lienhard tell more and looked at the USB stick on the desk. Lienhard's unfortunate friends in Chile were ultimately Meier's professional colleagues and they might have died in Chile for the data on this inconspicuous, small storage medium. As a scientist and a person, it was Meier's duty to carry on their legacy and act on their behalf.

The evaluation would take several hours, maybe even several days. Lienhard continued to talk to Meier who listened patiently.

Little did he know how fatal his meeting with Lienhard would actually be for him.

Chapter Twenty-Six

It was 3 am. After talking with Meier for several hours, Lienhard left the office in order to drive to Lucerne. He managed to hire 2 bodyguards for his safety and he found a hotel suite with extraordinary security measures.

Meier still was processing the data from the USB stick. He had remained stubborn and rejected Lienhard's offer for personal protection. "We're not part of a James Bond movie", was all he had said.

It would take some time before Meier could process the data to find out what discovery Lienhard's team had made.

The police and forensics found smearings on the walls in Lienhard's apartment: *The flat earth is bullshit! We believe in the globe.*

In addition, there were some personal insults and threats against Lienhard. The apartment had been searched by the intruders. No fingerprints were found, but an alleged letter of confession from the Globe Truth group, which had previously broken into the Flat Earthers headquarters.

Lienhard did not believe that any Globe Earthers fanatics were behind the attack. The three men he had seen did not look like any random fools. They were highly organized and had acted deliberately.

His desktop computer had been stolen. It was protected with an extremely complex code, but the right people would probably be able to crack the device in a few days or weeks.

In Chile, the serpentine road that led from the observatory into the valley had meanwhile been searched.

The car had been found.

It had fallen into a gorge two hundred meters deep.

No survivors.

The official investigation was slow, but Lienhard had enough money. He would find those responsible for the murder of his friends in Chile and hold them accountable.

Of course, Lienhard had thought about postponing the event or canceling it entirely. But then he understood that he really had to carry it out. He owed it to Pavel, José and Rodrigo. They had worked on his secret project for months. This could not have been in vain. He would present the project idea at the congress.

Chapter Twenty-Seven

IN THE EARLY MORNING HOURS OF THE NEXT DAY, WHEN THE SKY slowly changed from light-contaminated black to light-contaminated dark blue, there was a loud beeping sound. Meier jumped up from his office chair he had slept on.

His office looked chaotic; Everywhere labeled sheets and computer reports. The empty pizza box was still on the counter.

His computer program had just finished the evaluation and signaled this with a tone.

He froze as he looked at the data table.

That could not be true!

Meier knew that the data had not been verified. Errors were always possible and he could not inform his colleagues with this statistical uncertainty. The data that Lienhard had given him shook him deeply. But he would have to take his own measurements to verify everything.

Before he informed his colleagues and cry "wolf", he had to be sure. Nevertheless, he already printed out some tabular data, wrote a note on the slip of paper and put the folded A4 sheet in an envelope, addressed to a post office box that otherwise only Lienhard knew about. He went to the nearby post office and posted the letter as an express mail at the counter.

Then he got himself a hearty breakfast in a café near the observatory. He was completely overtired, had been working non-stop in his office for more or less two days. The air out here was pleasantly refreshing and he sat on a park bench and ate his sandwich, drank his cappuccino and enjoyed the mild morning sun.

Back in the office, he began to draft a report on the computer, which he wanted to present to his colleagues. Then he opened a new application and started further calculations. If all of this was true, this discovery would shake the world. He never thought that the Flat Earthers would ever surprise him. Now this was done.

At some point, however, the tiredness was too great and he nodded off right in his office chair and fell into a deep, long sleep. A whole day and night passed, and then an eternity.

He was still alive when the ambulance came, but there was nothing more that could be done for him.

Since he had not come to his regular lecture the next day, they were looking for him. An employee of the observatory finally found him sitting in his chair in his office. Further investigations showed that Meier had strange symptoms of intoxication.

His computer was confiscated, but it was password protected. It would take weeks before the IT experts would be able to hack the password via a brute force attack.

Investigations began and an arrest warrant was issued against Lienhard, who could be seen in the images of the surveillance camera in front of the Urania observatory.

But after the bomb attack on the congress, Lienhard could not be arrested.

Chapter Twenty-Eight

It had become evening and the dusk covered the landscape, also enveloping the caravan, in which Walser and Lienhard had been sitting for hours.

It was pitch black at the campsite. Only a small strip of light shone through the cracks in the closed caravan blinds.

At some point Lienhard had started to talk again after all and he had given Walser a short version of what had happened before the assassination attempt and also briefly told about his climbing accident and its consequences, even about his travel hypotheses.

Walser looked thoughtfully at Lienhard. He had now listened to him in silence for a long time and made notes, including some of his notes underlined twice or marked with question marks.

It was still unclear whether Lienhard had something to do with Meier's death. In any case, he found it very unsettling that the murderers of Meier and Lienhard's team had not yet been captured.

The safe was still closed.

Walser was afraid of its content. What if its content would be the last thing that Walser ever would see? Again, this really was Pandora's Box. Walser tried to hide his discomfort.

„You have to admit it", said Lienhard.

Walser shuddered. He felt caught out. "What shall I admit?" he asked.

„You don't really want to know whether the earth is a sphere or a disk", said Lienhard.

Walser relaxed again. "You won't change my mind about the globe", he said.

„This is so typical", said Lienhard, „it happens to all people who were globe heads and then became Flat Earthers. At first they thought it was a joke. Then, in order to debunk the flat earth, they did their own research and the surprise came. They suddenly had to admit that everything is completely different from what they thought." Lienhard got cheese, butter and ham from the refrigerator and fresh rolls from a small wooden box. It was already time for dinner.

„If I'm honest, I just don't care. In the end it doesn't make any difference whether it's a ball or a frisbee, so to say", said Walser. He helped set the table.

„But wouldn't you be shocked if everything were completely different?" asked Lienhard. He presented some fresh bread rolls. Apparently they were self-baked. They smelled wonderful. Walser took one. Lienhard seemed to have settled in well up here.

„I'm not a philosopher", said Walser and added some butter on the roll.

„Neither am I", said Lienhard, „But I am a man who found out that there is something wrong. In all these years I have seen almost all countries, but I never found the earth," said Lienhard and paused.

„The earh ...", repeated Walser.

„I told you about my *Brockhaus* list and about my problems getting back to everyday life. Worse than having to regain all my knowledge and worse than finding all of this so absurd, it was for me that nobody otherwise found it absurd ", Lienhard said and bit into his bun.

„Then maybe it's just your problem. Maybe you should just let it be and not bother other people with it," Walser said dryly.

„If it were that simple, we both wouldn't be here now. I wanted to know how other people see it all. So I made the Flat Earthers a success. If no one had a problem with the globe, then I wonder, why then thousands of people convert to Flat Earthers every day. Obviously there is something about the world view of globe earth that people don't like," said Lienhard.

„Maybe the problem is that you pretend that there is a big conspiracy. With your flat earth theory, you achieve that an old subject becomes explosive," said Walser and smeared the next bread roll. If Lienhard had wanted to poison him, he would have done so long ago, so these rolls were no longer important.

„Yes, you are right. An old subject is becoming explosive. In fact, this is exactly what I want", said Lienhard.

Chapter Twenty-Nine

LIENHARD HAD MADE GOOD USE OF THE TIME AFTER HIS MANY travels. He was quickly promoted and elected to the squad of the bank. As an expert in finance, he gave regular lectures and he enjoyed being successful.

Many companies booked him for lectures. One day in autumn, he was asked to speak at an international seminar for financial planners. The event took place in a small seaside resort in Turkey.

Lienhard left the hotel around noon on his day off and read the A4 sheet on the front door. *Watch today: SUN ECLIPSE !!! From 11:30 AM to 3:15 PM. Buy our special SUN GLASSES at the reception desk. Ask Mr. Arslan.*

The organizers had timed the one-day seminar so that the participants on the following day had the opportunity to watch a solar eclipse if they were interested, which would be clearly visible from Turkey.

Lienhard hadn't looked at his to do list for a long time. But the term "sun eclipse" within his *Brockhaus encyclopedia* still was pending. So for him it was obvious that he would not miss that opportunity.

Outside the air was already shimmering. It was a hot day, but the tourists didn't seem to mind. Many of them had escaped the cool autumn weather in Western Europe in order to enjoy a little more summer here.

The beach was already well attended, people were bathing in the water or sitting on the beach towels. Lienhard looked through the solar eclipse glasses at the sickle covered by the moon. It wasn't long before the total solar eclipse.

Suddenly a murmur went through the crowd. The entire environment appeared in a strange light. The colors appeared so intense. They were different. The brown of the wodden walkway to sea appeared darker. The green of the trees near the beach had changed in many ways. Everywhere appeared colors of an unprecedented intensity. He had never seen anything like it.

Lienhard shivered, it had become noticeably cool. The air smelled of evening, damp, earthy.

Something flew very close to his head, probably a bat. The solar eclipse gave this exotic, airy holiday resort something bitter that he could not explain. It reminded him of the pictures of Edward Hopper.

There was a strange mood in the air. Lienhard felt kind of degraded by the epic process.

It occurred to him that in North America the warriors of an indigenous American tribe called *Chippewa* used to shoot burning arrows at the darkened sun during a solar eclipse in order to rekindle it.

He noticed other peculiarities that this event now brought with it on this formerly bright morning: there was a sunset on the horizon. Some stars, perhaps planets too, seemed to have lost their way into the daytime sky. Birds that had just been chirping fell silent. Then, at the speed of a jet, a big shadow raced over the landscape and covered everything. All became dark. It was creepy.

Although Lienhard knew better, he was startled and for a moment he felt the same intention as the warriors of the Chippewa tribe. Now the crickets also fell silent. The night was here. The crowd was speechless for a few moments. Only a couple of children could be heard crying.

At some point the first, bundled rays of light were visible, which made the sky light blue again.

Another murmur went through the crowd, then cheers, and a few people even applauded. After a few minutes everything brightened noticeably and soon there was the blazing afternoon sun as if nothing had happened.

The crowd dispersed again and the rising heat drove the people into the water.

He looked around: Now the area was again what it had been before, devoid of severity, an average tourist place, lit by a normal sun, the sun of the south.

Finally it was again a groovy destination for all sun seekers who wanted to escape the spring cold front of the north. The heaviness was gone.

Lienhard began to sweat again in the blazing sun and went back into the shade of the trees.

He looked at the holiday bungalows in the distance, at the palm trees in the midday sun, then walked a few hundred meters through the hinterland.

The sky shone deep blue through the treetops. The sky had now degenerated again into a backdrop for what was really important; the stories of the people.

Somewhere behind the bushes he heard tourists chatting and laughing. Everything was back to normal.

The crickets chirped again.

A few sparrows fluttered out of a tree back into the ordinary sky.

The ground almost simmered in the intense heat and there was a smell of tree resin. Lienhard walked along the beaten path. With every step he stepped on dried pine needles, which rustled and gave way under his feet. Small lizards scurried back into the bushes when he approached.

He inhaled the salty, heavy air carried by the sea wind. From a tennis court in the distance he heard the regular sound of tennis balls bouncing the tennis rackets. He smelled the gradually evaporating sun cream on his face.

Everything was fine again, well known.

Above there was the bright blue sky.

The moon, now visible again, looked flat and pale.

Nevertheless, with the naked eye he could see the Sea of Silence on which Apollo 11 had landed at the time. So this was a foreign celestial body on which people had set foot many years ago.

He couldn't tell what was bothering him, but something felt wrong to him, something was wrong.

The earth is flat, he suddenly thought.

Chapter Thirty

EVEN DAYS LATER AFTER HIS DISCOVERY, HE FELT DISTRACTED. IT didn't work to get back to normal.

Even during the whole flight from Antalya to Zurich he had been looking out of the plane window. He had tried to prove to himself that the earth was not flat out there. It seemed that he could see the curvature of the globe, but he did not believe that he was looking at the curvature of a planet. In addition, he knew that he only saw the world now through this thickened, rounded glass. Anyway, whatever he would now see through would be irrelevant. Because in fact, the flat earth that he meant had nothing to do with the curvature.

On the next Saturday morning he got a rental car and first drove to a lake nearby. It was beautiful weather. The sky was blue and opaque and some white, fluffy clouds were populating the sky. Lienhard walked randomly over the fields that surrounded the lake. He looked at the vast country. The air already smelled of autumn. One could feel absorbed by the landscape as it seemed so big. Only the night or the look at the globe on the table would ever question the vastness and indicate that there was something else than this small world. But else everything outside this world seemed like a fairy tale. And maybe this even was the greatest legend in the world: the globe.

Lienhard was still stunned by the thought that had seized him after the solar eclipse and while looking at the moon.

$$* * *$$

He decided to make a short trip to Lucerne. About two hours later, in Lucerne, he just caught the *MS Winkelried*, one of the tourist ships on Lake Lucerne. Together with pensioners, a group of Indian tourists and a handful of Swiss families with different dialects, he sat on the outside deck. He gazed at the water. Impenetrable and viscous, the turquoise water sloshed at the Vitznau station. It looked like a light-flooded pudding.

"How deep is it here to the bottom?" asked a maybe 6 year old girl next door to the grandmother.

"Deep. Very deep", was the answer.

"How deep? A hundred kilometers?" asked the child further, whereby the grandmother owed her an answer.

Lake Lucerne with its mountain range seemed to him like a bulwark, a citadel in the middle of an uncertain world. There was no universe but just a cheesy tourist destination. The fjord-like bays that surrounded the deep blue lake, the wooded surroundings with the massive mountains: it was sweet here. For a moment he understood the foreign tourists who found this Swiss kitsch cute and pretty.

When the evening sun was low, the ship finally docked again on the quay in Lucerne. He looked at the lake one last time. Cumulus clouds over Uri.

After a spontaneous visit to a nearby cinema that was showing the *Matrix* trilogy, he went back to the car. There had been a thunderstorm. He saw leaves on the wet ground and it smelled of damp asphalt. It started again to rain. He hurried to the parking garage and when he got into the car rather drenched, a taxi driver in the parking lot next door called out to him in a good-natured tone: "The weather's bad, isn't it?"

Lienhard laughed and said: "Yeah, darn rain."

But actually he loved the rain. When it rained, the world seemed even more closed and far from anything giant and monstrous: car tires were splashing on wet asphalt and the cloudy sky was concealing the stars. Everything was so normal and urban.

He drove along the streetlights. Measly illuminated human world, he thought. He drove and drove through the night on this straight road, always straight ahead without reaching a destination.

Damn flat earth, he thought.

Street signs kept appearing as well as lonely, orange flashing traffic lights at the intersections, which were all deserted. The world seemed alien. No poetry could have comforted him in this place of the ancient night.

Without the daylight, he thought, this place lacks any harmlessness or comfort, because everything that was taken for granted had now flaked off like road paint from the asphalt. Beneath the urban surface, there was revealed a celestial body.

When he left the Lucerne town sign in his car, he suddenly didn't feel like going back to Zurich and instead he took the next motorway exit heading south, without meaning and without purpose. Switzerland was so small and you could drive through this mini-country so quickly. Through the now open window he smelled the spice of the freshly mown meadows.

After a while, he felt strange. He thought: what a desolate journey, what an inhospitable landscape without any poetry, and when he thought back to Ms. Reber, he felt damn lonely at that moment.

Loving the wrong person was a stupid, stupid art, but only when there was unjustified hope. This had long since faded. The tension that something would follow after their meeting in Paris had been gone for years. He was even a little relieved, because any affection he still had for this person would no longer take itself seriously, but only apply to this person, pure, without claim, without expectation.

He didn't know whether he believed what he was thinking, but he felt a deep connection with this person, a benevolence that was greater than him. The week before he happened to see a BBC broadcast in a hotel room in Turkey about the loggerhead sea turtle's 15,000 km journey, and then something about beetles and orangutans. At the same time he had felt a strange sympathy for all living beings, could not escape it, this unbearably fragile, innocent life over which he wanted to hold his hand. An ode to the world, an ode to Frau Reber and her gentleness.

It was now 1:30 am in the morning and he drove and drove on and on, chaotically, aimlessly. At some point he drove through the Gotthard tunnel that canalized him to Airolo. Then he drove on until he finally found a gas station in the neon light at a motorway exit near Lugano. A bright island of bliss. The shop smelled of freshly baked bread and machine coffee. A pop song came from the speaker.

He bought a few drinks, a small cheese and ham sandwich and some Cailler chocolate bar with a roll, plus a fleece blanket. Also he took a coffee from the machine.

He found a parking lot nearby. He munched on his sandwich in the semi-darkness, sipped the steaming coffee from the paper cup and looked at the dangling key of his ignition over his knee. His car: a 220 hp powerhouse that could be started at any time and moved from here, a vehicle that accelerated from zero to one hundred in 8.5 seconds, if necessary. He liked the non-committal, of being free to go now wherever he wanted on that planet. He gazed at the stars.

It turned into a restless night in which he only found a feverish, superficial sleep. He constantly saw the flat earth in front of him, and woke up with a headache and a furry feeling in his mouth. Once he woke up, it was just before dusk. He wiped his hand over the steamed-up car window and looked out the window at the white spaces. Besides his car there was only another one. A white Fiat Panda was parked right next to his car that was a space-consuming, black Lexus RX 400 h. It seemed to him like if in the middle of a dark jungle a small animal was trustingly and cuddly looking for the safety of a larger, good-natured animal that happened to be sleeping in the same place.

The next morning, after a coffee and a pretzel in a bar, he drove to Locarno and saw a sign: *To the planet path*. He was curious. It was a 6 km long path that began right at the Lido and led him to the municipality of Tegna, always along the river. During his hike he remembered the little girl on the Lake Lucerne steamer and her question about the depth of the lake.

He started with the sun and went on and on. Mercury, Venus, Earth, Mars were reached quickly, after a few minutes. Jupiter took a little longer. Saturn was then quite near. But Uranus was a long time coming, a very, very long time. Lienhard marched and marched and he wasn't sure if he had somehow missed Uranus. Then, after about an hour, he found it. Fifteen minutes later, there was Neptune.

An information sign said that you would have to hike another 40,000 km for the closest fixed star.

Chapter Thirty-One

THE SOLAR ECLIPSE HAD THROWN LIENHARD COMPLETELY OFF course.

The first thing he did was quit his job.

He created an annual plan for all cosmic events: solar eclipses, lunar eclipses, Mercury transit and also swarms of meteorites, etc.

In order to prepare for his big task, he started with the dimensions again. So he decided to reconstruct what he had seen in the planet path in Locarno.

As a makeshift, he made up his own solar system. He took an exercise ball from the bedroom and labelled it as the sun, then he left the sun in his apartment and went to the neighboring parking lot about 40 meters away. There he put a hemp seed grain. That was Mercury. Twice as far away, he placed a small, brownish marble: Venus. Another 20 meters away, he placed a larger blue marble on the floor. The earth. The head of a pin turned into a moon. He took 80 steps and put a cherry pit on the floor. The Mars. A little more than half a kilometer away from his apartment, he placed a foam ball. Jupiter. He took a pétanque ball for Saturn and put it down about a kilometer from his apartment. Twice as far away, he placed a ping-pong ball (Uranus). Another kilometer away, he put another ping-pong ball on the floor. Neptune.

But to visualize the Milky Way, the scale was no longer sufficient. Even for the next fixed star he would have had to march 40,000 km. So he had to change the scale. Now the pin was the solar system. He went to the soccer field and it was the Milky Way. He stuck the pin in the ground in front of the gate, because here was the outer Orion arm of the Milky Way.

But actually he also had to reduce this reduction again. The Milky Way was now the pin head and the observable universe would have covered a radius of 443 km.

In the course of one day he was able to exercise the different proportions.

Lienhard reminded himself that the *Milky Way* belonged to the *Local Group*, which had a radius of around three million light years. In turn, it was part of the *Virgo supercluster*, to which several thousand galaxies belonged. Diameter: 150 million light years. It was dragged along by the supercluster *Hydra Centaurus*, which was towing an even more gigantic gravitational source, the *Great Attractor*. And this in turn was only part of an even larger structure, the filaments and voids, a network of perhaps a trillion galaxies.

Afterwards, Lienhard created some additional models. This time, he used sand. In the course of a day he was able to gradually exercise through the various proportions.

Unfortunately, he could not approximate the absolute number of stars in general with this trick, because he had read somewhere that all sandy beaches in the world might not have enough sand to represent this. So after an hour he gave up, left it all, and went to the nearest travel agency. The very next day Lienhard flew to Muscat via Dubai. Once there, he walked for a fortnight with Bedouins through this wasteland, always along the edges of the Rub al Kali desert. He climbed over the endless mountains of sand, rested at her foot, walked around her, measured her circumference in steps, but all of this without progress. So he chartered a propeller plane and let himself fly over the dunes for hours in order to better assess the breadth and dimensions. Below him, there was the monotonous pattern of ocher-colored hills and deep shadows, all the way to the horizon. So he looked down at the huge, sometimes 300 meter high, massive dunes and tried to imagine the individual grains in them, stacked suns.

Chapter Thirty-Two

Much time had passed since Lienhard's stay in the Rub al Chali desert.

Lienhard strolled on the lime-tree-lined *Bahnhofstrasse* in Zurich.

It was Friday, just before 5 p.m. It was still quite light. Dusk would soon fall.

The colored lanterns of the city trees, through which the big candle had glowed so warm and red in the late afternoon, would soon go out.

He went to the quay on Lake Zurich and looked at the undulating surface. There he sat down on a park bench, right next to a fountain, and watched the cars and trams go by.

How strange it was when he watched the streets and the pavements, the houses and the people in their cars. All of this was so normal. But in fact it was an urban deception. It was a surface that had been built on a former no mans land. About 240 million years ago the soil around Zurich consisted only of granites and gneiss, then came the ocean and now Zurich was located here. Now, nothing revealed that it all was built on a planet. It was a domesticated earth.

When the scent of spring wafts towards you, the cherry blossoms sway in the wind, the fluffy clouds are carried away across the sky, who would want to think of the strange world beyond this planet?

Everything was so wonderfully earthly and turned towards the everyday world, the earth is a celestial body, but above all a world on its own.

But when in a few years the space would have been made accessible for travel and one could travel through the filaments and voids, it would probably show that none of this would count more than the warm laugh of a loved one.

And yet he was drawn there, to this strange world that would always remain inaccessible to him.

If for once one just paused, maybe on a quiet city Sunday, when there was little traffic and one stopped on the sidewalk of a street and watched how the wind rushed through the city trees and one saw cyclists here and there, how they comfortably rode on the asphalt, if one then thought for a moment where this was all happening: it was strange.

This contrast seemed somehow magical to Lienhard. The giant filaments and structures with a size of billions of lightyears. And here this beautiful fountain in the park.

It was just a matter of the direction of the gaze. Considering the filaments, Zurich looked very surreal. How could there be such an urban place within a galaxy? The other way around, if one looked from here, from this city, to the sky: Wasn't the universe just a legend? He didn't know what seemed more surreal to him: the filaments or rather the city in view of the filaments.

Lienhard stayed on his park bench until it was dark night. Tomorrow morning he would fly to Cape Canaveral.

Chapter Thirty-Three

Lienhard had briefly told Walser about the solar eclipse and what happened after it.

„And then we made the Shuttle flight", said Lienhard.

„With the Simulator?" asked Walser.

„No, in reality. We flew around the moon. That was damn expensive", replied Lienhard.

„Who could pay for such a trip?" asked Walser.

„A whale", said Lienhard.

„A whale?" asked Walser.

„Things have been going well for me in the past few years. I had five million –", said Lienhard, but was interrupted by Walser. "You had five million of what? Five million of value? In Swiss francs? For that little money, you couldn't even send a postcard to the International Space Station."

„No, it was not a value of 5 million. It was the number of coins that I had because I was a crypto whale. I had cryptocoins – plenty of them. So I had 5 million Bitcoins: 5 million pieces. I sold everything when the price was going to the moon," said Lienhard.

Walser knew that, so far, Bitcoin was worth almost a million dollars apiece.

„And what did you do there flying around the moon?" asked Walser, without going into Lienhard's Bitcoin story.

„For two days we flew to the moon, circled it for one day and then flew back for two days. That was all", said Lienhard.

„That was all?" Walser asked with a laugh.

„Yes," said Lienhard simply.

„If you don't show me proof, I won't believe a word you say", said Walser.

„I can prove everything," said Lienhard, „also there was a data leak afterwards. That's why Meier had found out about it and confronted me."

„Why did you fly to the moon?" Walser asked.

„Because I was able to", said Lienhard.

„Did you want to see the flat earth with your own eyes?" asked Walser.

„No, on the contrary", said Lienhard, "I wanted to free the earth from its two-dimensionality. I wanted to get rid of the picture of the earth. I wanted to finally see something real."

He put the blue marble on the table.

Chapter Thirty-Four

WHEN, AFTER THE ATTACK ON THE FLAT EARTHERS CONGRESS, Lienhard's wounds had been adequately cared for and he had known that all the injured would be treated, he went into hiding immediately because the perpetrators would continue to hunt him. He had to stay away from other people, otherwise he would endanger them.

He knew by now that he had been bugged weeks or months before.

Everyone he had contact with was the focus of the attackers, including Ms. Reber.

He had warned her by email, but she had sent him a message that she wanted to meet him in Seville. He already knew where.

After her email reply she was no longer available and so he could not prevent her from travelling to Spain.

It was 4 p.m. The first guest he was now in the same flamenco bar as then, but under a different sign, as the hunted. He looked at the premises: everything looked exactly as he remembered it. He took a seat on the same bench as then.

The police investigation had been slow so far. Neither the attack on the Flat Earthers Congress nor the murder of Meier could be explained by the circumstantial evidence.

Even the small bomb had generated a considerable pressure wave and hurled wood and metal parts through the air. A piece of metal was then stuck in his knee and his face was deeply scratched by splinters of wood flying around. Even though both bombs had been placed right next to him, he got off lightly. The first bomb hadn't gone off in the first place and the second had misfired due to shorting.

Since the attack, the media have published new revelations and speculated a lot.

He would tell Ms. Reber everything and she would finally stop looking at him as a weirdo. Your signature at the time at the collection of the CERN employees had hit him very much. Still, it wasn't about him now, but about her safety.

The room filled up and Lienhard kept an eye on the entrance. He would recognize her immediately, even in dim light, when she entered the room. His bodyguards had been positioned and monitored the area around the house.

Time passed and it was soon 9pm. She should have been here long ago. He kept waiting. The flamenco songs changed, but Frau Reber stayed away.

Even when the last guests had left and the bartenders started to put the chairs up on the benches, mop the floor and turn off the lights on the stage, Lienhard sat and waited. He waited all night.

The daily News mentioned it casually the next day. On past Tuesday afternoon, a delivery van had been driving at excessive speed on the road from the airport to the city of Seville. As a consequence of this, the man rammed a taxi with full force from the side and then committed a hit-and-run accident.

The local taxi driver and the female passenger, a Swiss woman, were killed immediately. No doubts due to the further details. Some TV pictures of how the helpers were cleaning the street from the splinters and pieces of luggage. One of them was helplessly holding something in his hand that he had picked up from the floor, a red book by Camus.

Chapter Thirty-Five

It was said that Ms. Reber was still conscious when the ambulance came. She was able to move, but just stayed on the ground and looked at the sun as if she wanted to take as much light as possible with her.

After losing all these people, Lienhard felt a strange kind of disillusionment. He felt so weak. The days after Mrs. Reber's accidental death passed quickly and surprisingly easily, so that Lienhard was disappointed with his own composure, but in the days that followed, the pain showed its power.

In theory, such a pain could have had a kind of cleansing function like a thunderstorm that cleaned the air. But Lienhard did not want to feel relieved. He also avoided melancholy and sentimentality, because he wanted nothing to do with any bittersweet superficiality.

What was actually horrible remained very subtle. The actually horrific could not be described, it came and went and taught Lienhard true loneliness.

He knew that beautiful things might happen again in the future, which he would witness or even be involved in, but it would remain insignificant. No luck would ever reach him again, no matter how edifying. A deep powerlessness enveloped him and he wondered who he was doing all this for at all.

Sunsets of great beauty and fluffy clouds like a painting had often presented themselves to him since then, as well as the cuteness of small cats and the smell of summer rain, and also the sound of the wind in the reeds, as if fate wanted to console him. And he took everything grateful to, but thought to himself: the world, a cold beauty.

His whole agenda had now been tainted and taken to absurdity by the murder of these people.

José was almost 23 years old, a young math genius who got bored at university and therefore signed up for Lienhard's project. Rodrigo, with a PhD in astronomy, had become a father for the first time two months ago. Pavel, who had contacts with various space companies, had been Lienhard's ally from the very beginning and had initiated the secret project with him. Lienhard also thought of Meier, who had helped him despite his feud against the Flat Earthers and who was now also dead because of his commitment.

On the other hand, he didn't think much about Ms. Reber. Otherwise he would have gone mad.

With all his money, Lienhard could not only have circled the moon a thousand times, but also could have bought it, but there was no one who would have swapped Lienhard's money for these five lives.

Ms. Reber had followed her appointment as humanitarian helper to India and he had supported her aid project anonymously, discreetly, blindly and with the necessary restraint. She never had learned that the money for her foundation had come from his pocket. Just knowing that this person was doing well where he was had reassured him all these years. But now Mrs. Reber was no longer in India. Several times he had felt panic. He didn't care about The Flat Earthers anymore, he didn't care about his secret project in Chile anymore, he didn't even care about the explosive discovery of his astronomer friends anymore.

The flat earth no longer interested him.

He shipped his caravan to the alp and lived for four weeks at this resting place like a hermit, saying, doing and thinking nothing that had been so important to him before and for which he had fought.

On the quiet evenings he stood outside on the campsite, saw the illuminated valley. Then he had some very bad ideas when he looked into the black abyss in front of him.

There was only scorched earth left in his life.

How could anyone want to save the whole world when he could no longer save the one he loved?

Lienhard was a Midas king of filth, had wanted to save the world and, in the process, let his friends and confidants fall to dust.

It was a Sisyphean task to grasp the irreversible, the final in it.

Lienhard went to himself, meditated and looked at the panorama appreciatively, but it wasn't as if he simply did yoga and found himself again. The herbal tincture for the wounded animal had not worked miracles as society would have liked to see it. Society quickly perceived grief as a nuisance. He didn't come back enlightened and purified from the mountain but only in silence.

He had been harmed and would remain so and he would never understand or forgive how something so beautiful, such a beautiful soul, could go out of the world. A soft, compassionate being that had been casually razed to the ground by a titan's heel. Ms. Reber, that clever and kind person that had devoted all its existence and thinking to quantum physics as well as to the protection of the weak, had been destroyed like by an evil child that casually crushed a bug.

Time does something to us.

Nothing good.

He knew that after all, betwee him and these people there would be a bond forever. It was just important that sometime things happened and beings had their own story, their own sequence of causality.

After all, one couldn't expect more from this planet and once one was dead, a few million years would pass like the blink of an eye.

A few weeks later did he pick up Meier's A4 sheet of paper again. There would always be blood on that paper. The lives of good people had been ruined because of the numbers on this paper. But he knew that with every day that now would pass, the document would be devalued in terms of its explosiveness and usefulness, while the blood would forever stick to it.

He remembered his odyssey back then to Ticino, the moment when he had thought of the loggerhead sea turtle's 15,000 km journey. And he immediately suspected that he probably no longer loved the world, but still liked it enough to protect it in honor of the lost.

Chapter Thirty-Six

3:19 AM. *STAR TREK*. WALSER WILL HOLD OUT ALL NIGHT. SCIENCE fiction films increase the acceptance of extraordinary ideas, he once read. Even B-movies are ok.

Our societey has a useful division of labor: the nerds fight their way through the thicket of future with the machete and pave a few trails for the masses.

Like the hippos in the Okavango Delta.

... Lucy, Limitless, X-Men.... ET, Infected, The Thing from Another World, Under The Skin, Skyline ... A Space Odyssey, Interstellar, Ad Astra, Mission To Mars, Ender's Game, Pitch Black - Planet Of Darkness, Solaris ..... Back To The Future, Timeline, 12 Monkeys, Looper, Timerunner, Clockstoppers, Timecrimes..... Screamers, Terminator, Blade Runner, Automata, Westworld ...

Walser would think of other titles, but he is too tired.

4:15 am. Platypuses on National Geographic. Platypuses. Simply platypuses. There is nothing to add.

5:30 am. ARD tv channel: The world of the winds. Mistral - The ruler of Provence.

In the meantime his heavy tiredness had been replaced by a jaded feeling.

The need for rest intensifies and if he is not more alert he will fall asleep next. Everything he sees alienates him in a strange way. Everything just seems crazy to him the more he stares at things.

This whole world seems absurd to him, this bustling life on the spinning rock. It is perhaps the same effect that he sometimes experiences when looking at language, when he writes a newspaper article and a word suddenly seems strange to him as soon as he reads it several times. Then some words seem absurd to him, it can actually hit any word. No word is safe from it. Word.

He gets a cheese sandwich out of the fridge and brews another coffee. He'll stay awake as long as he can. He doesn't want to press the switch-off button and sit in front of a black screen. He does not want to take a break from the panopticon.

It is not good that one day all the sights that the television offers will suddenly come to an end. Even random zapping is better than a black screen. No, under no circumstances does he want to turn off the television, the main thing is that something is happening on the screen and is reflected on our retina.

He thinks: I like the tv. I like that blue flicker that contains a whole world in it. I want to absorb the world now, hold on to it and always participate in it, not lose sight of it. The television should run forever. It is huge that all of this is inevitably ephemeral, but sometimes I am happy. I ate bananas, oranges, and cake, I knew many, I went swimming in the lake.

6:45 a.m. Walser learns on the BBC: Armadillos have a fine sense of smell.

He thinks: You think you know the world. But then suddenly it is a alien to you. It comes and goes and grabs you by the neck like a predator. It attacks you, sometimes when you look at it by a glass of wine, sometimes just casually in a certain moment. You think you know the world, but then it alienates you and you wonder how you could ever have looked at the stars unsuspectingly. I don't know what frightens me more, the inhuman vastness of space or the the former impartiality of my gaze.

He remembers an old black and white cardboard photo that he recently saw in an antiquarian bookshop in Zurich. He had almost bought it. The picture, from 1901, was slightly yellowed with a sepia effect and showed a young cat with a tilted head and an expression of curiosity on its small face. And the caption said: *A wonder in her eyes.*

Once, many years ago, when he was walking past a taxi in Zurich with the driver's door open, a scent that came from the leather of the car, but also from the cardboard fir tree and fir wood perfume dangling from the front mirror. At the same time, there was something trivial and yet also special about this smell and he was happy to remember it since.

Another time, some time before sunset, he was working on his Bachelor's Biology thesis in a rented study room, which was located in the tower of a disused brewery. Then he looked outside and saw the glowing evening sun in the open window of an approx 1 km distant skyscraper reflected. The bright red, the pinching light, it wasn't snappy enough to damage his eyes. He looked there for a long time without being able to detach himself from it, and he was amazed at the peculiar beauty of this reflective window. He couldn't get enough of that. There was something so warm about it.

Is he imagining something because of the tiredness or does he feel a slight jolt in the caravan? Is there a strange noise, a hum? He could go outside to see, but he stays seated.

The earth is flat. He now understands.

The sun should rise soon; his waiting at dawn. The light shines strangely through the caravan window at the golden hour.

He wants to see the world forever. With everlasting compound eyes.

His hands grip the warm coffee cup tightly and he takes a deep breath.

There exists, on this early Wednesday morning in October, a

small, precious world, not realizing how beautiful it is, how delicate it is.

133

On the dunes you'll never forget it.

small, precious world, not realizing how beautiful it is, how delicate it is.

133

Chapter Thirty-Seven

„So this is your flat earth", said Walser, as he took the blue marble in his hand.

"The earth is flat - not literally but metaphorically. Back then, the solar eclipse showed me that for me the universe was always just an old wives' tale, just like all the other objects in the Brockhaus that were out of reach from the start. There was that rare occurrence that affected the sun and the moon and I understood all astronomical facts about it. But at that very moment I grasped that it actually had nothing to do with what I knew. Because of the solar eclipse, I realized that all of this was just an entertaining spectacle for me, an abstract process, but nothing that showed me that the earth was also that little dot in space, as everyone said. Earth was not a ball that I was living on but a platform on which our stories took place, a nice place with trees and houses and meadows. The earth was flat. Just like the universe. All just a flat picture, two-dimensional. So I helped the Flat Earthers. I wanted to free people from their rigidity. So that they could see the world with new eyes. So that they question the usual picture and see the real object behind the picture."

"So what was then the aim of your mission in Chile and the Antarctic?" asked Walser.

"We collected data," said Lienhard, "in order to establish a completely new visual representation of the earth and the solar system. With hundreds of probes and a completely new way of showing the earth. A very special live stream. These novel images would have been accessible to all and would have revolutionized humanity's view of the world. "

"But still, these would only have been pictures. But at the same time you critizise pictures", said Walser.

"That's true," said Lienhard, "that's why every participant in the congress would have received a free shuttle flight from me. A free lap around the moon. I wanted to change space travel from something that is only available for a handful of people to something that is for everybody. My plan was to democratize the view of the earth. This is what I wanted to announce that as news at the congress. But then the bomb came."

"But who attacked you then?" asked Walser.

"It was because of the data my team found. Killer squads were sent by someone who knew the data that I gave Meier. In fact, I only received his letter after the bomb attack. So during the congress, I was completelly clueless. There would have been no reason for the bomb. But those who already knew the data and had observed us, wanted to liquidate me, my team in Chile, Mr. Meier and Ms. Reber

"But for which dates would murder be worthwhile? What did you see when you saw the earth from the moon?" asked Walser.

"The data that Meier sent me will change the world – they are in here in the vault," said Lienhard.

"And what about the killer commands?" asked Walser.

"My employees tracked them down, including the people who hired them", said Lienhard.

"Then are we safe now?" asked Walser.

Lienhard became silent for a moment and took a deep breath. It almost seemed as if he had to collect himself in order to be able to believe the information himself that he was now about to reveal to Walser.

"When my friends in Chile were evaluating the real-time representation of the planets and taking various measurements in order to plan the project to orbit the moon, they happened to also find this data – " said Lienhard and startet to open the combination lock on the safe. He took out an A4 sheet of paper. It was the sheet that Meier had sent him. He put the paper on the table in front of Walser who read it through several times. In addition to tabular data, it had the name of a huge asteroid.

"The sheet shows the variables and the possible scenarios, including the probabilities. And the extent," said Lienhard, „the scientists equate it with the situation of the dinosaurs."

Walser turned pale as a sheet.

"And what now?" Walser could not think of a wiser question about this danger of biblical proportions. He swallowed hard.

"Of course we immediately informed the Federal Council. But they already knew. All governments around the world knew. They just did not publish any breaking news on this issue. In fact, there was an international pact of absolute secrecy. Everyone was silenced, even whistleblower websites. But there were also some circles who wanted to make sure that really nobody knows. So they had sent killers after us."

"But what now?" asked Walser helplessly.

"The problem cannot be solved as easily as in the movie Armageddon, but without any hope people go crazy, plunder, murder. Soon share prices would plunge into the abyss, deals fail, trade and production would slow down, work would be stopped, Economies would collapse and mortgages are no longer would be paid. Well, even governments would collapse and instead, anarchy would reign. The whole world would collapse before the real thing happens," said Lienhard.

"And now what?" asked Walser again.

"Governments have their own way of dealing with such scenarios. But in case that all plans fail, then just think of the films Deep Impact and 2012. Only a small part of humanity would be evacuated: presidents, super-rich, Nobel Prize winners, fertile people, young people, and so on, "Lienhard said.

"And you?" asked Walser. A new question had finally occurred to him.

"Back when I was able to act again after bomb attack, I joined forces with other super-rich. Together we invested all of our assets to find alternative, crazy solutions. We hired physicists, nerds, visionaries, weirdos and technology freaks. They were free to mention any crazy idea. We accepted every imaginable science fiction solution for further investigation", said Lienhard.

"Were you successful?" asked Walser with a heavy tongue. His mouth was dry as dust.

"That will show, because no one was prepared for something so real, although mankind has already talked about it in dozens of disaster films. We can now only wait and see whether our plan takes effect."

Walser emptied his water glass, then asked: „But why do you need me?"

"I need you as a chronicler," said Lienhard, "against oblivion and against a flat earth. I'm more or less broke now. The money is in the rescue plan. Live stream and moon landing are canceled. I need you for the time after that. If there is a time after that. Otherwise we don't have to worry about the flat earth. "

"Meier noted a date on paper," said Walser, unusually quiet and hesitant.

"Yes. The date he calculated back then is exactly right: everything will be proven tomorrow morning," said Lienhard.

"Tomorrow already?" asked Walser and was startled.

"Yes, tomorrow", Lienhard repeated in an unusually mild voice.

"I understand", said Walser and understood nothing. He felt an emptiness in his head.

The two men sat together at the dining table for a long time, talking. Then Lienhard prepared new sandwiches for both of them and Walser made notes for his story.

Some time later, Lienhard Walser gave the key to the second caravan and pointed out the good TV satellite reception with two thousand channels. Walser nodded.

"All the best," said Lienhard and shook hands with Walser, whose hand trembled even more than his voice.

"Thank you, I wish that to all of us," said Walser.

Lienhard looked at him, almost like a father looks at his son, although they were only a few years apart in terms of age, and he patted his shoulder almost like a father.

Chapter Thirty-Eight

Walser left Rebers caravan. It was now night outside.

It was drizzling and the night sky was overcast. He looked from the hill at the lake and at the lights of the unsuspecting city in the valley.

Wild animals could be heard from the forest and the temperature was no more than maybe two or three degrees. He was cold, but he stayed outside for a long time, took a deep breath and inhaled the cool, moist air. He listened to the sound of the rain and just enjoyed the moment.

All these people who didn't know anything about the place out there, about the Damocles sword. Hopefully they would be able to read his report in the paper this week.

He looked up to the sky. Above, briefly released by the cloud roof, he could see a few dozen inconspicuous points of light were here and there. And if one looked closely, there were even a few myriads.

After a while, Walser went into his trailer, brewed some tea, wrote his story and turned on the stove and the television.

Epilogue

"Hike to Keitum. The first trees for weeks; what we call landscape: the green forgetting that we live on a cellestial body. On the dunes you'll never forget it for a moment."
Max Frisch, Diary 1946 - 1949.

ISBN 978-3-9525443-2-7